SWEET CONQUEST

SWEET CONQUEST

It seemed that nothing could go wrong for Sandra on her birthday when she was bubbling with high spirits, heiress to a fortune and engaged to the most attractive man in the district. But everything did go wrong, when she was taken to hospital after an accident and discovered that her fiancé only wanted her money and was secretly in love with her beautiful cousin. As rich girls could never know if they were loved for their money or for themselves she vowed that she would make it difficult for any man wanting to marry her.

Sweet Conquest

by

Quenna Tilbury

Dales Large Print Books
Long Preston, North Yorkshire,
BD23 4ND, England.

British Library Cataloguing in Publication Data.

Tilbury, Quenna
    Sweet conquest.

    A catalogue record of this book is
    available from the British Library

    ISBN   978-1-84262-868-3 pbk

First published in Great Britain in 1980 by Robert Hale Ltd.

Copyright © Quenna Tilbury 1980

Cover illustration © Stephen Carroll by arrangement with
Arcangel Images

The moral right of the author has been asserted

Published in Large Print 2011 by arrangement with
S. Walker Literary Agency

Dales Large Print is an imprint of Library Magna Books Ltd.

Printed and bound in Great Britain by
T.J. (International) Ltd., Cornwall, PL28 8RW

ONE

Sandra Stevens threw back her head, and let the wind tear through her hair. It was good to be alive on a day like this, even if the bike was old and nobody knew she had taken it out. Happiness like hers has a bursting point, and the big silent stone edifice that belonged to her great-aunt had a smothering effect on a day like this, with weather like this outside. Besides, to stay in Darley House on her birthday was unthinkable!

Eighteen today, she thought, as she pedalled round a bend that would give her the first sight of the sea, and Yelstone village. Behind her was Brunchurch, a strait-laced county town which exactly suited Great-Aunt Evadna. Brunchurch society, she severely told her niece, was ideal for a young girl like Sandra, who was orphaned, and should really try to cultivate suitable friends. Great-Aunt Evadna still clung tenaciously to the time and manners when she was young, and didn't care if she did seem to be eccentric. When you were as rich as elderly

Miss Darley, you can afford to be anything you like, and you can make that tiresome comment 'Money talks' come true.

Sandra hated it, and hated Darley House and her life there, and really honestly liked going about in the 'uniform' of an eighteen-year-old – faded ragged-edged jeans, cotton top, no make-up and her straight brown hair all ruffled up by the wind. What did looks matter, so long as you were in the pink of health, had a good skin, and weren't ugly? In spite of her lack of grooming, Martin loved her. He had said so.

Martin... She made the name sound like music in her mind. The wind whistled it in her ears, and the sound of the trees creaking and rustling breathed the name. Martin Byrne. Martin Frenstoke St John (pronounced Sinjun) Byrne, who had a titled relative somewhere in the family and was as high-class as Great-Aunt Evadna could wish for. But somehow Miss Darley always seemed to look as if she had been sucking a sour lemon when she spoke of him. Sandra didn't understand it at all. You would think Great-Aunt Evadna had something there to be really pleased about, but no, all she would say was that handsome is as handsome does, and never mind the young man's family, they hadn't two brass farthings to rub together, and he was only after the Darley money, which had been made in trade.

Brief anger flashed through Sandra as she cycled through a water splash across a country lane, and felt her bare feet tingle with the cold as the clear water splashed over them and dripped along the dry surface of the lane, on either side of the wet tracks her tyres made. Everything was fun today. It was good to be alive. She forced herself to remember that Great-Aunt Evadna was seventy-five and had to be pushed around in a wheel chair by a starchy nurse all day. How awful not to be able to tear about, and risk a heavy shower of rain because of your health! How dreadful not to walk in deep snow, be afraid of slipping when the ice crackled underfoot in the lanes in winter; never to be able to venture out without gloves, nor touch the daily winter miracle of hoar frost on withered leaves, and see the edge of the waves freeze on the beach. Never to get up at dawn in summer to inspect the roses and find the smallest newest bud housing a dew drop. Audrey said Sandra was mad to take notice of such little things, and why didn't she be sensible and go to London to the big shops and get herself a decent appearance, which would be sensible.

Audrey, the other great-niece ... pretty and well-groomed and everything a man could wish for, but ... Martin didn't love her. It was Sandra, his beloved hoyden, as he called her, that Martin loved. He had told her so last night, and asked her what sort of engagement ring she would like. It would be, in the end (she knew) the family ring, a heavy old-fashioned cluster of diamonds and rubies. Just for a moment she had wished they could have gone together to a jewellers and chosen a single diamond. It would have been fun to choose it together, and to know that Martin liked it too. But somehow Martin kept aloof from such things as prices and visits to shops.

This was a thing which worried Sandra: what Martin's family would think of her. They lived abroad. Aunt Evadna had commented acidly that it wasn't a smart thing so much as an expedient thing, since they just couldn't afford to keep Byrne Place open. But they were going to re-open the place. They were going to come home and get it ready in time for the engagement party, and the wedding, which would be a big white one, with all Martin's relatives there, and Audrey chief bridesmaid.

Sandra stopped her mad journey as the road plunged into Old Hangings Wood and stood leaning against a rail, thinking this out. It was something that lay beneath her happiness, clouding it a little – the sort of thing that ought to be got out and thought about. Except that she didn't see what thoughts would do about it. Privately she considered that no amount of money spent on trying to groom her would make her into the sort of bride that Martin's family would want. She wouldn't fit, she thought, with a little frightened flutter. It didn't matter that she had gone to good schools, or that she was the heiress to both the Darley and Tugwell fortunes; Darley's dog biscuits and the Tugwell range of kitchen appliances, were not things that Martin's family would want to talk about. Sandra, the realist, knew that. Which only made Martin's love for her more precious. But how would she fit in, she wondered? It was not an argument that would take up much of her time on her 18th birthday, she suddenly acknowledged to herself. His family wouldn't accept her, but he wouldn't give her up. So they would buy a nice (little) house with her money and settle down to bring up a nice family of boys (like Martin) and harum-scarum girls (like herself) and with her money, which she generous acceded could do the job, she would bale out Martin's family, so they could again live in Byrne Place as they used to. There, it was simple, and all settled! She remounted her bike and tore off through the woods, bumping along a path pitted by exposed tree roots and big stones, a hair-raising ride which she needed to get the taste of that fierce mental struggle out of her mouth. She hated pretensions and what you were supposed to do with money, as against what you would like to do. And she wasn't at all sure that she was going to like Martin's family. But he obviously adored them so she would try to like them for his sake, as he tried to like Great-Aunt Evadna for Sandra's sake.

Now she had sorted all that out, she could give herself up to thinking about Martin, who was, according to Miss Darley, much too good looking and suave and charming for any young woman's husband. Sandra swept that aside as just one of Miss Darley's acrid comments on one of her bad days, and remembered Martin's kisses...

It lasted to the top of Old Hangings Hill, a hazy dream of Martin's tender hands on her face, and on her ruffled hair, Martin's fund of lover's talk which was as imaginative as descriptive, and could be filed away to be taken out and dreamed over in bed at night, when out of earshot of Miss Darley's fierce conversation when she was in pain or just disgruntled with her limited world in an invalid chair. But it definitely wasn't suitable for dreaming over, when you should have your wits about you cycling down Old Hangings Hill. She had whizzed past the permanent sign: 'Black Ice – Extreme Caution' which never seemed to prevent accidents in bad weather, and she had taken the sharpest part of the hill before she discovered that her brakes weren't working.

Now the posts with the red reflectors had passed, and the ditch, leaving only the bank of long grass and weeds on either side, and mercifully no other traffic. She weighed up her chances of jumping off, but left it too long, because she remembered that motorists had a habit of throwing out into the long grass of the bank a variety of rubbish including beer tins and pop bottles which sometimes broke against the hidden big stones. So it was the second sharp bend that was her undoing. The bike hit a boulder and threw her to the left, and the road – with a solitary cyclist on it – veered sharply down to the right. Both bikes converged, but mercifully the riders went into different directions. The bank, hard with the force and speed of the impact, hit her and winded her, and for the moment she blacked out.

The other cyclist, with a scratched face and a trickle of blood running down from a cut on his forehead, was bending anxiously over her, as she opened her eyes. She struggled to get up but he held her by the arms, and said, 'Take it easy! Do you always come downhill like that?'

She studied him, and closed her eyes. 'Ugh! I've got a thumping headache!' she complained. She had intended to leap up and look at the damage to the bike. It belonged to the new girl in the kitchen, who would have to have a brand new bike bought for this. Miss Darley always bought something brand new to replace any damage they had done to other people's belongings.

The young man impatiently wiped his hand up his face, glared at it, and said, 'Disgraceful! What will my aunt say when she sees me?' and that seemed to afford him much amusement, and served to cloak (Sandra was to remember later) his swift appraisal with deft hands, for broken bones. He decided she hadn't any, and to judge by the way she scrambled to her feet, no internal injuries, though he made the perfunctory suggestion that she should be taken to hospital for a quick check-up.

'Don't be silly, I'm all right! I'm always doing this – falling off a bike or some such thing. I'm tough!' she told him. 'And my head's not aching so much now. Besides, whoever heard of going to hospital on one's birthday?'

'People do, so I'm told,' he said dryly, and got up and stood looking at her. 'You must come home and get cleaned up, anyway, and then we can see how you are! I'm Richard Norwood – staying with my aunt and uncle at the vicarage,' he explained, as he picked the odd twig off her jumper and his own (torn) jeans. 'But do be advised and don't come down that hill like that any more!'

'You only want to keep me to practise your First Aid,' she told him crossly. 'What do *you* know about broken bones and internal injuries. Get you!'

'Come on, you must be in need of a cold drink, anyway. I am. I'm parched, and my aunt's parsnip wine needs to be sampled to be appreciated.'

'Lemon squash will do,' Sandra said

primly, and felt a little light-headed. 'How am I going to ride that, for goodness sake?' she asked in dismay. The bike was a twisted mass.

'Leave it there. Someone will pick it up later. You can ride back on my seat – I'll push. The vicarage isn't far, through the Spinney – short cut.'

Miss Darley didn't know the clergy of Yelstone. She was 'seen' at the big church in the town, and that was the church she fed her wealth into. One of the things one 'should' do, when one belonged to a family like theirs; Sandra had been brought up on that understanding, and had never questioned it. Even Audrey made a perfunctory appearance at church once a month, helping push her great-aunt's invalid chair. Sandra often wondered why, as she wasn't likely to benefit from Miss Darley's Will: they had always been given to understand that. Something to do with Audrey's father having displeased Miss Darley, but Sandra's mother having been the apple of the old lady's eye. Sandra often mutinously wished it were the other way round.

With this sort of background, she was rather surprised when she was taken into the big sprawling Rectory at Yelstone. The house looked cosy and much-loved, even from the outside. There was a casually successful garden and the vicar's wife, coming to the door to meet them, having seen this unusual sight from the vicar's study window, had a most sweet face. Sandra had formed a sort of permanent idea of what a vicar's wife should look like: hatchet-faced, like their own vicar's wife, or thin and acidular, like the curate's sister. Richard said cheerfully, 'Hallo, Aunt Marion! We had a bit of a tangle up on Old Hangings Hill, and I've brought her home to be cleaned up, but no bones broken!'

'Really, Richard, you really should be more careful! It doesn't mean to say there will be no bones broken just because you are–'

What she had been going to say was lost in Richard's cry of alarm. 'Aunt! Look out – Buster's in the strawberry bed!'

His aunt turned, with an exclamation of alarm, and rushed after an overgrown puppy who was chasing a kitten, to the danger of young strawberry plants growing near a warm sheltered wall. Richard grinned at Sandra. 'Come on, let's find some water and soap, and then some tea.'

'I can't impose – your aunt looks too busy,' Sandra protested.

'Don't be silly! She'll be offended if you don't stay now,' he said firmly.

'Mr Richard! Look at the state you're in!' An elderly woman with a huge white apron, emerged from the back of the house, carrying a tray of coffee and cakes. 'You're all alike! Bullying others to keep fit and getting into that state yourself – look at the blood on you!'

Sandra now had it firmly fixed in her mind that he was some sort of First Aid person. She grinned at his embarrassment.

'All right, Trudy, we'll go and get cleaned up. And could we have some of your lovely chocolate cake?'

'Not so fast! I'll take the young lady up to the bathroom,' she said, putting the tray down, but the vicar's wife came in from the garden, a puppy in one arm and the kitten nestled into her neck, and said, 'Don't worry, Trudy, I'll see to them both,' and again Sandra was caught by the sweetness of her smile. 'What happened, really, Richard?'

'Tell you later, Aunt Marion,' he said, and vanished in the direction of the vicar's study and the tray of coffee.

The bathroom was a small room converted. Sandra, who was used to a tiled affair opening off her own bedroom, pink with all the trimmings, was enchanted with this no-nonsense washing place. The bath was old-fashioned but big, and the green stains from the taps down to the plug hole in no way detracted from the novelty of it all. Ivy was trying to push its way through the slightly opened sash window, and the lino had seen better days. But it was clean and smelt of the good super-fatted soap and towels hung out to dry in the fresh air. Ordinary white towels. Sandra smiled broadly. 'What a nice bathroom!'

'What's your name, my dear, and how long have you known Richard? The vicar will ask me and if I don't know, he'll say I'm getting vaguer every day!'

'I'm Sandra Stevens and I only met Richard today when I bashed into him. I hope his bike isn't in the state mine is. Still, mine was old when I started out this morning, so it doesn't matter much.'

'Richard must pay for the repairs,' Marion Vendall said firmly.

'Oh, no, please don't let him because then my aunt will get to hear of it, and she makes rather a fuss. I've got a friend who will mend it for me, so not to worry.'

'Then that's all right,' the vicar's wife said serenely. As her life was laced with the friendly services of people repairing things in return for similar kindnesses, this didn't sound strange to her. Sandra shrewdly felt that it would go down better than airily saying it belonged to the new kitchen maid, who would be made a present of a new bike to compensate for a member of the family taking liberties with other people's possessions.

After a quick wash and a comb through her short thatch of hair, Sandra happily went downstairs with Richard's aunt. 'I felt a bit shaky at first but I'm fine now,' she said.

'Did you let Richard go over you, just to make sure?' Marion asked, already looking for signs of the puppy and kitten in mischief again.

'Yes, that was all right,' Sandra said easily, and thought how doting relatives were so proud of someone in the family taking up First Aid. It had been the same with a school friend of hers. The worst bandaging in the world, but just to mention her St John's Ambulance classes was to put her doting parents into transports of pride and delight.

The vicar was not at all like his wife. He was a big, pleasant faced man with a very shrewd pair of eyes, which at once made Sandra feel that Darley's Dog Biscuits was written in letters of fire all over her.

She said quickly, 'I'm a stupid thing who ran into your nephew on Old Hangings Hill. I don't deserve his kindness in bringing me back here to get a wash and brush up, and I really shouldn't be intruding in your coffee break, in your private study, too!'

The vicar was enchanted. 'My dear, my own family never remember they are intruding in my study, so why should you? Sit down by me and tell me how you came to unseat Richard, who is reckoned to be quite careful on the roads?'

'Not when you have a bike with no brakes coming towards you, Uncle!' Richard protested, and there was general laughter, while the chocolate cake was passed round, and if the vicar looked as if he were trying to remember where he had seen Sandra before, he got little chance to voice his wonderings because Richard and his aunt kept up a cheerful cross-fire of talk about puppies and kittens, a Miss Kellett who did the flowers, the woman in the second cottage who sold cheaper and better eggs than the local farm, and what the cowman had been suffering from on Midsummer's Night. Sandra would have liked to listen to all that, but the vicar talked to her about small craft (but didn't explain why or what his interest was) and the sexton's little mistake (but didn't tell her what it was) and then the others heard, and there was delighted laughter; a positive shout of laugher from Richard, who, Sandra thought, might be rather fun. Martin would like him ... or would he? This was another thing which worried her lately. Martin showed little inclination to get to know her friends, or to like what he had seen of them. Was he not going to mix with them?

'Then will you?' Richard's Aunt Marion asked, in the tone of a person who has already repeated the question once.

Sandra started. 'Oh, I'm so sorry, I wasn't listening. I expect I will, though, whatever it is!'

'No, my dear, that won't do!' the vicar said firmly, amid laughter. 'Never, never rashly promise to do a thing or agree to a thing, without knowing every little thing about it. Bless me, I don't believe you even know what you're letting yourself in for? Have you ever kept pet animals?'

Sandra remembered the way the house-keeper had looked, when she had been offered a Bedlington terrier once, and the second housemaid had handed in her notice at once, on the grounds that if miss were even thinking about a puppy, then it was as good as here, and think of not being house-trained! Sandra said, 'Well, actually no, because the … the person who cleans up wouldn't … wouldn't…'

'Exactly! There you are, you see!' the vicar exclaimed. 'And that gives you your answer, Marion! I told you you'd have to keep the last of Dorrie's litter. Personally I don't mind an extra animal around the place. They're rather jolly, to my mind. Better than putting it in a raffle, poor little beast. Think of it, it might be won by the Horrockses!'

'Oh, no!' Marion said, blanching. 'Oh, dear, I hadn't thought of that! In fact, I didn't really think of the raffle. That was Trudy's idea, because of raising more money for your fund. I believe she'd put me in the raffle if she thought it would draw customers.'

'Now what a good idea!' the vicar said wickedly, and joined in the laughter against his wife.

Warm, the atmosphere in the vicarage. Not just warmth of house and furnishings, but of people. Sandra would have liked to know them all better. She hated it when it was the polite time to go, especially as the vicar came to the door with her, his arm round his wife's shoulders. Richard brought round a disreputable old car from the back, and said he was going to take her home and no protests.

She waved and smiled hard at them as they drove out of the vicarage gates, and then she sat in frozen silence trying to think of a way out of this new pickle she had got herself into. As surely as if he had said so, Richard wouldn't want to go on knowing her if she admitted to being the niece of rich old Miss Darley at Darley House. And in spite of being engaged to Martin, she did want to go on knowing Richard and his lovely relatives. They would be such good friends to have, in the days ahead when she foresaw that Martin's family might cause her to be not exactly happy, to put it mildly.

She said, carefully, 'Look, it's awfully kind of you, but I wish you'd just drop me at the bus stop. I can manage.'

'Where do you live, Sandra Stevens?' he asked gently but firmly.

'I don't mind you knowing, but I think I'd better not tell you because I think you're going to insist, from kindness, of course, on taking me up to my front door, and that will be disaster, because then they'll know about

24

the bike. You see?'

'Oh, lord, yes, how clumsy of me! I hadn't thought of that!'

'I think, on second thoughts, I'd like to be dropped in Brunchurch High Street, if that won't take you out of your way. I'd forgotten the bread.'

Her aunt would have gone stiff with horror to hear her say such a thing, Sandra thought, with wry amusement.

Richard said, in horror, 'Don't go to the bakers in the High Street! Goodness, what a pity you didn't say so back at the house – it's Trudy's baking day. You could have taken one of her loaves. She cooks for the week!'

'I couldn't do that!' Sandra was shocked. 'Besides, I didn't make it clear. My aunt is on a diet. I meant I wanted the Health Food Shop.'

'Well, that place sells a lot of rubbish, for a start!' he growled. But he gave in when he saw how distressed she looked. 'Smile again, girl! You really have got the most unusual and taking sort of smile! I've never seen my aunt and uncle go overboard for any girl I've brought home before.'

'They were really nice people,' Sandra said warmly. 'I liked them too – very much. It was a most enjoyable visit, really, in spite of the way we met.'

'Come again!' he urged. He wasn't looking at her, giving all his attention at that moment to getting round the new oval roundabout that fed traffic more or less tidily into the network of main roads through Brunchurch. So he didn't see her abject dismay, for Martin was standing easily beside his new low-slung sports model, and she had just remembered that he had said he wanted to show off its paces to her today. He was to have picked her up at the time she had been careering down Old Hangings Hill…

Her heart began to beat unevenly, as she recalled the look on Martin's face. She could almost hear him saying: 'Who the devil was that shabby type you were with in that ghastly old car?' Tears stung her eyes for no good reason. She felt she wanted at all times to think of Martin as being the best and kindest of men, but she knew instinctively that he wouldn't like Richard Norwood, nor the way he dressed, nor the patch on his forehead, nor the old car he was weaving in and out of the traffic, and she herself was aware that she liked Richard very much and wanted Martin to get on well with him. Who was it said that it wasn't one's friends that were a headache to one, but the fact that they wouldn't mix with each other?

'Don't bother about taking me any further,' she urged. 'I can see a friend on the pavement there. Just put me down here. I can get out quite quickly,' and she opened the door.

Richard said something to her, stopping her, she thought, but she dare not wait any longer. She began to slide out, hastily shut his door as a motor-cyclist edged past on the nearside of the slow moving car traffic, and then shot herself through to the pavement and lost herself among the shopping crowds there.

Up through a narrow alley and into the next street, Sandra was able to approach the road where Martin had been standing by his car. He had gone now, of course, but a taxi was crawling along the pavement, and she got in, hiding her untidy self away from people who would know that she was the dog biscuit heiress from Darley House.

Great-Aunt Evadna had her bad days and her good days, but this was a special day. She had been expecting to lunch with her niece on her eighteenth birthday and she was hurt when only Audrey appeared. Sandra came in just as they were finishing.

Sandra was late because she had remembered there would be the meal with Great-Aunt Evadna, and she hadn't got anything she considered decent to wear. She had stopped at a little shop down a side street off the High Street, and bought a dress, very much like the one the vicar's wife had been wearing. Simple, a shirt-waister, one that Sandra felt suited her better than the ones made by the old lady's personal dressmaker; expensive material, impeccable taste and cut, adding up, Sandra thought mutinously, to very dull garments indeed. This was the first dress she had bought in her life. Off the peg! She had raced upstairs, evading the people from the kitchen, who were taking in the special dishes the old lady had to eat, and the special dishes Audrey was convinced she should eat, as she was a weight watcher. The kitchen staff entered a conspiracy to dress up both diets to look like normal and beautifully served meals, and it took time and they got angry if people came in late to sample their masterpieces.

They glanced at the new dress, too. Sandra felt a flash of anger that people should have a pre-conceived notion of how an heiress should dress, and marched into the dining-room with her head up.

Great-Aunt Evadna sat at one end of the long table, and Audrey at the other. Sandra's place had been cleared away, by her great-aunt's orders, no doubt. The old lady looked up and said flatly, 'But we have almost finished!'

'I'm sorry, Aunt Evad!' Sandra said, rashly forgetting that her aunt could be extremely nettled with that shortening of her name. 'But it's my birthday so don't, please don't, be cross with me today! I am sorry I'm late, really I am, but it wasn't my fault. Something happened to me!'

'It would do!' Audrey murmured, half under her breath, but the old lady put her fork down at once, and looked concerned. She seemed to have shrivelled a little today, Sandra thought confusedly, as she pulled up a chair close to her and began to tell her about the need to get out and feel the wind through her hair. Fussily the staff began to set a place in front of her. Sandra waved them off, Miss Darley indicated that they should proceed. 'You must eat, child! Aren't I always telling you so?'

'Oh, never mind food, Aunt darling,' Sandra said. 'I was having a lovely ride down Old Hangings Hill and there was another cyclist coming up–'

It was a mistake, of course. Well-trained as the staff were, they were listening, and although they didn't look at her, there was an infinitisimal pause in their movements, which meant that they had at once put two and two together, knew she had borrowed Milly's bike, and that it was probably no further use now. Sandra never did things by halves.

The old lady said, 'Eat first, then tell me about it afterwards,' and instructed the servants to bring a normal sized meal, that she would see her niece ate. The three of them sat in silence at the table while this was done, and only when they were alone again, did the old lady speak.

'Now, Alexandra, first things first. It's your birthday. It is the first time today that I have had a chance of seeing you, so here is your present from me. And I believe Audrey would like to give you something, too.'

Sandra felt chilled, both by the use of her full name, the rebuke in the way her great-aunt had started the ceremony, as it should have been performed if she had arrived for the ceremonial lunch in the proper way, and the tone of the old lady's voice. It would be the emeralds.

Sandra confusedly opened the case. No

gift wrap – Great-Aunt Evadna thought such things vulgar. This had been brought from the bank, in preparation for this day. Sandra had known about it, long before, and had forgotten about it. Well, why not? Other girls might remember a gift of an emerald set – necklace, bracelet, long ear-rings – and be thrilled to bits, but for Sandra it was an embarrassing gift. She never wore jewellery. Now, to use this lot, she would have to be poured into a gown, a model gown, and be painted over, as she contemptuously thought of the exterior given to Audrey by expensive beauty parlours. It was a plot, and she had to play along with it because, for some remote reason, her aunt had chosen her, and not Audrey, to be the heiress. A reason that had little to do with the two girls, which wasn't fair, because Audrey wanted to be rich, and would have done justice to her aunt's fortune. What was the good of someone like Sandra inheriting all that much money?

The case lay open in front of her. A large leather case, velvet lined, with all the items arranged in their special indented places. They had been cleaned and re-set, she guessed. And she remembered belatedly that her aunt had decided she no longer disapproved of the new age for becoming an adult, so this 18th birthday was really quite a big occasion. All that had happened to her that morning paled into insignificance.

Audrey quietly put a jeweller's box beside Sandra's plate, planted a formal and quite insincere kiss on her cousin's brow and said, 'Happy birthday, anyway,' and slid back to her seat.

Sandra felt a little sick as she opened it. She didn't believe in taking gifts from people you weren't friends with. She herself never bothered to quarrel with people or even dislike them. The world was a good place. But Audrey was quite special in that she had the ability to make even someone like Sandra come near to quarrelling with her. It was as if life would lack excitement if Audrey hadn't got someone to disagree with, and to make the disagreement sharp, never to be forgotten. An event, in fact. Sandra loathed it, and feared Audrey and her queer ability to make a person behave out of character. She opened the jeweller's box.

In it was a workmanlike watch, plain of face, shock-proof, the sort of gift nice ordinary people had. Sandra warmed to it, having dreaded an attempt on Audrey's part (including mortgaging every penny she might have put by) to procure a gift to go with the emeralds. She hadn't.

'It's just what I wanted!' Sandra said, seeing nothing funny in saying what the maids might have said to such a gift.

'I know,' Audrey agreed coolly. 'I happen to know you broke the last one on the pier last Spring. I couldn't afford a dress watch, and anyway, you're getting one from Martin, so what?'

There, she had done it again, Sandra thought, not able to look up because she couldn't see clearly. Martin's gift had been a surprise. He was coming over this afternoon with it. Now it was no surprise. Audrey had not only spoiled that for her, but now she was to ask herself how it was that Audrey knew about it.

Great-Aunt Evadna said, 'Well, well, child, now you're of age. Put your baubles away, and eat your food. It's cooling already! Then tell us what outrageous things you got up to this morning. Will I never make a lady of you?' she sighed. Just the sort of sigh and just the sort of thing said, that one might expect from Great-Aunt Evadna, who still lived in the past.

The rest of the meal passed unexceptionally, because the old lady made small talk with an effort – it was her great-niece's big birthday – and Audrey was good at small talk, which she turned on like a tap. Nobody would think that behind Audrey's cool calculating grey eyes, (discreetly made up so that the old lady shouldn't object, and also because Audrey had a theory about unskilfully plastering make-up on) there was bitterness, because she hadn't been chosen as the heiress. Audrey chatted, made openings for the old lady to talk about things that interested her personally, and generally helped things along until the coffee came, and then the nurse came and took the old lady away in her wheel chair.

Old Miss Darley's apartment was a self-contained one on the ground floor, opening by a ramp into a rose garden, which had beyond it the walled garden with the pool and fountain. Peaches grew on the walls of this sheltered spot. The old lady loved to sit there and dream back over the years when she had been young, and men had courted her. Her brother, who had been responsible for the enlarging of the firm and the amassing of the fortune she alone now enjoyed, gave her the emeralds on her coming of age, and the diamonds on the day of her engagement to a penniless peer. Miss Darley said goodbye to him in the garden where the fountain was. He had been too proud to marry her for her money. He had the wild idea of sailing to the Indies to make his fortune, so he could come back and fetch her on his own terms. But when he had made his fortune, he forgot about plain Evadna Darley, and married a pretty girl from an aristocratic New England family, and hadn't returned to England. But Miss Darley remembered him, and always told herself that if her fortune had been larger, she could have been sure of him.

She went there today, to think about Sandra, and to reflect how odd it was that here was another plain one, who didn't really care about money, only love. How that child loved that scapegrace Byrne!

She wished that Fate hadn't sent Audrey into her care. It would have been easy to lavish all the money and advantages on Sandra, and to have been reasonably sure that she would get a husband that way. It might have been easy enough if Audrey had been plain and unaccomplished; then she could have been happy to make them joint heiresses, a fortune apiece. Then they could have liked each other, with no jealousy. But it wasn't easy to apportion money between two girls, when only one had so much by way of natural gifts and talents. She sat listening to the threading of the fountain's tinkle, with the music from the piano above, in the ornate music room. Audrey showing off at the keyboard. She had said she wanted to learn to play the piano, and had thrown herself into it whole-heartedly. Sandra had just grinned and agreed that it was a fine accomplishment, but while there was fresh air outside, Sandra wasn't going to waste time and effort doing what could be acquired by buying a record in a music shop. That was Sandra: no eye towards the future. No sense of values, where accomplishments were concerned. What if the money went, as fortunes sometimes did vanish? What would Sandra have, to keep her going? What was she capable of doing? How could she earn a living?

The old lady felt quite unwell at the thought, and decided to get this marriage with the Byrnes over and done with. At least Sandra would be respected in the district, married into that family. What if the old lady herself didn't like them? What if the family didn't care for Sandra? They would have to be nice to her, because of the money.

She fell asleep. Presently, after the manner of the old, she awoke, not knowing what had disturbed her. Two angry voices were cutting the air. She glanced up. It would be from the music room, but from where she was sitting in the shade, she couldn't see the open windows, nor could they see her from the music room. But their irate young voices cut the air.

'You make me sick!' Audrey said clearly. 'Pretending you think people don't mind you going about looking like a tramp!'

'Well, they don't! It's only you and Aunt Evad who make a fuss!' Sandra stormed furiously. Audrey must have been being unpleasant for some time, to cause Sandra to get worked up, the old lady thought, her heart beats quickening. A row bothered her, made her feel queasy and fluttery in the chest.

'Let me tell you, you're something of a laughing stock!' Audrey flashed.

'I'd rather be laughed at for being natural than made-up like you are!' Sandra said quickly. 'And I'd rather be me and let other people live as they want to, and please themselves, than be like you, always picking on others because they don't believe in the same things as you do!'

It swayed, that quarrel, now loud-voiced, now a low grumble that was incomprehensible, sitting as Miss Darley was, two gardens away from the house. She thought miserably of the kitchen staff, who would undoubtedly be unashamedly listening. She had never been able to make Sandra realise that if you kept servants, your life was an open book to them. Audrey knew this, and usually kept her voice down, but Sandra would never allow that other people were so interested in her that they had to pry and peep through keyholes. A simple soul, Sandra, the old lady thought irritably. She should be less simple, having in mind the amount of money that would pass into her hands in the future. That was another thing. Sandra could never be made to realise that money was not just a pleasant thing to have, but a trust, a thing to be nurtured, watched, worked on, a thing that employed many other people, a thing that must be enlarged, made to work for itself, not allowed to dwindle or run away. It was a monster, the old lady thought, in sudden clarity of vision, or perhaps because she was in the defeatist mood of allowing that her money was her master. She was too old and too tired to be bothered with it, she thought, in amazement and despair.

The quarrel flared up again, suddenly, like a dying bonfire that the wind has suddenly returned to lick into flame. 'Who are you kidding? Martin's no fool!' Audrey said bitterly. 'Okay, he's going to marry you, but it's your money he wants. Did you think – could you be so naive as to think – it was you he wanted?'

A shocked silence greeted that. Sandra at last rallied her forces to say steadily, 'I think you're feeling sick about something. Something's upset you today and you just want to take it out of someone. I agree, it must be galling when you know you look so well-groomed and lovely, to see a handsome man like Martin fall in love with someone like me...'

Audrey laughed, a little wildly, with some despair in it. 'Oh, save me! Correction: he's *marrying* you, not in love with you!'

There was a longer silence after that, then Audrey, shocked at what she had done, said quickly, urgently, 'Look, you brought this on yourself, but I've maintained all along that someone should tell you how things are. I mean, you couldn't, you wouldn't – even you! – be so batty as to think you could make someone so suave and impeccable, fall for you? Think, Sandra! You really are the end! Most of the time you look downright shabby, and sometimes not even clean! Well, when you've been out for a walk, and come bursting in – I mean, if you'd just stop to think! Hide yourself, slip up the back stairs and get cleaned up, don't let him see you like that, if you *must* go for long walks and get messed up! But you don't! You let him see you at your worst! Sometimes I think you just don't care!'

'Say it again … that he doesn't love me,' Sandra said, on a queer note.

'Oh, you must know! It can't come as a complete surprise to you! He and I – well, I let out that I knew what his present to you was, so that must have made you guess? *Surely!* Well, doesn't it stand to reason?'

'That he should love you, and still want to marry me?' Sandra asked, in a stifled voice.

'Don't you know him at *all?*' Now Audrey was shocked. 'He's a stickler for doing the right thing! He's engaged to you, he'll marry you! Besides, he *has* to. He needs the money. His family are hanging on to the idea that it will come, and soon. Everybody is!'

'The money,' Sandra said. The old lady couldn't hear now, and with difficulty she turned her chair and got it a little way nearer. It exhausted her, the effort, but she had to hear. This was the framework, the life's work, she had set up, and it was going sour on her. She was frightened, but it was no use calling out for someone to help her. If she did, it would make a scene, and the girls would terminate their quarrel to come and see what was wrong. No, she must get nearer herself, somehow.

Audrey said, on a higher clearer note this time, 'You are the heiress. Nobody's going to deny that. And his family are panting to get their hands on the money. They have to, poor things. Oh, don't look so scornfully at me because I sympathise with them! They do have some decency in living, they have a pride, which you haven't. He'd have to marry money somewhere, so as you're handy, you'll get him as a husband. Isn't that something? Presumably you'll want a family, (you always say you want babies) and you'll get that…'

'Don't! Sandra said sharply. Audrey had trespassed far enough, and she couldn't even see it.

'I suppose you'll tell Martin about this row?' Audrey said, after a moment. 'I wish you wouldn't, but I suppose you will. Not that it will do anything. He loves me and I – oh, can't help ourselves, I suppose.'

'And when I marry him, what then? Am I to sit at home, and know he's out with you, and you're both in love, and I'm just the …

41

the wife?' So much bitterness and shock was packed into that, that Audrey could only look helpless, and shrug. She hadn't meant to have this row. Sandra had nettled her, being so self-righteous about liking the simple things of life. And now she had created a monster, and what was she going to do? A monster that would leer at her every time she looked at her cousin.

'Sandie!' she said urgently, holding out an imploring hand and not even noticing, so that the gesture looked oddly touching and not over-dramatic. 'Let's not be bad friends?' she pleaded.

'You think we could be happy, the three of us?' Sandra said, in a hushed voice. She looked oddly white under her even tan, so that Audrey wondered if the shock had been too great.

'Yes! Yes, we could! We all like each other, don't we? I mean, I might come and live with you, help you...' Audrey trailed off, before the enormity of the suggestion she had made.

Sandra laughed, a low bitter little laugh not like her at all. 'Coming-of-age day! My word, I've come of age, all right. I've grown up with a vengeance – if you did but know it! But I'm not so naive as to think we three could live together in the same house, Audrey! No, I tell you what I'll do. I'll pretend this hasn't happened. I won't wait for Martin to come here with his present – I'll go to see him. And I'll just convince myself that you've been being catty at my expense, which I think you have. I know Martin. I don't believe he could have carried off such a deception. I'd have known if he'd been in love with someone else. Personally I think you're just about as bitter and selfish as you've ever been, and as jealous as always, of me. Only you forgot to hide it. I wish you hadn't forgotten.'

'Where are you going, to find Martin?' Audrey asked her.

'Now where would I go?' Sandra said, her voice getting more reasonable every moment, as if she were clearly brushing the whole thing to one side.

'No need to go anywhere, my dear. I'm afraid I'm here,' Martin said, from the doorway.

TWO

Audrey was the one who ran to his side, held on to his arm, looked imploringly up into his face. Sandra stood staring, fascinated. She ought to have realised...

Audrey's face softened and she smiled at Martin, and Martin glanced down at her, not smiling, but yet with a softness in his eyes that there had never been for Sandra herself. In that moment, she didn't require any discussion, any explanation. It was all there. Just the look of the two of them. Audrey was aglow with her feelings for Martin, and somehow they were more mature than Sandra's own feelings. Hers, she saw suddenly, were a schoolgirl's love for a hero. She hadn't really been touched by passion, as no doubt Audrey had. Bathed in love, she thought, and looked away, as if she were looking at something she had no right to see.

She stared out on the gardens. She could see the top of the fountain, over the rosy redbrick wall, but not Miss Darley, who was in the shadow of a big trained bush, and had toppled over in her chair, sheet-white, eyes closed. The shadow of the bush hid all but the front wheel, but Sandra wasn't looking at the ground, but at the general picture of hot pulsating sunshine and heady blossom smells, the shrill noise of birds on a day in high summer, and a general don't-care attitude on the part of Nature. All's well with the world, the summer day was shouting, and everything in it echoed that sentiment, but in the house, the old unhappy stone edifice known as Darley House, she herself was following the usual pattern of the Darleys rich from trade – her world had shattered, slipped apart, and was as empty as a barrel on its side.

She heard Martin tell Audrey to go out of the room while he talked to Sandra. At least, she heard him say, 'Go away, Audrey,' and the words themselves were uttered with a caress. She marvelled that his speaking voice could be so different to Audrey, yet he had sounded so romantic when talking to Sandra herself. The difference, now she had seen both, was sharp and clear. With herself, he had been playing a part, like an actor on a stage. Playing a part with cleverness, with deep interest, enjoyment even, and he had made it convincing. But with Audrey just now, he hadn't been playing a part. He had been a young man shaken with helpless love for a girl he would not be able to marry, because she hadn't got the money his impoverished family needed.

Sandra watched him. She had no words, in which to put all the jumbled thoughts, the fears and the amazement, the hurts and the chill feeling of being frighteningly alone, after having felt cosseted, cherished. She thought in confusion that there is nothing quite like thinking you are beloved, and then find that you are not the one who is loved, but only on the outside looking in. She stood waiting for something to happen next, because since she had seen the way he had looked at her cousin, she knew that the hastily thought up speech of a few moments ago would not now do. They were just words, unnecessary words. Words to let him prove the truth of Audrey's accusation, but had he not proved the truth of it within seconds of entering the room? Her brain felt frozen, so she just stood and waited for him to make the first move.

Somehow he pulled himself together. This wasn't the way he had wanted it, at all. He hadn't wanted to fall in love with Audrey. He knew he wasn't in love with Sandra, but he knew his duty to his family, and he hadn't questioned that, no matter how unhappy his own future might be. And now all that he had done was to appear to have behaved badly.

He walked slowly towards Sandra. She was afraid he would take her into his arms, but he didn't. He couldn't have. She looked alien, in that dreadful dress (the sort one of the maids might have worn for best) and there was a stranger looking out of her eyes, which bothered him. The warmth of her smile had gone; her lips seemed frozen. He wondered if she had sustained a worse shock than either he or Audrey realised. He hadn't wanted this to happen either.

'I don't know what to say!' he said at last, rather helplessly.

'I'm surprised,' Sandra said quietly. 'I would have imagined, from the build-up that Audrey gave you, that you'd never be lost for the right word, the *bon mot,* I believe it's called.'

He flinched, and his anger came to his rescue. 'I don't think you've any call to take that attitude with me. After all, you kept me waiting an hour and I saw you with some dreadful chap in a terrible old car. Not quite what I would have expected from you, Sandra.'

It was almost comical. He had said practically word for word what she had imagined at the time he would say! But it was no laughing matter. 'He was giving me a lift back, after I'd been involved in an accident.'

'Oh, is that all? Then I'm sorry. Truly sorry. Tell me about the accident.'

'So you can check that it isn't a fabrication? I was on a bike, so was he. We crashed, on Old Hangings Hill.'

'Oh, is that all? Bikes!' He lost interest. His friends had car accidents, never bikes, Sandra told herself bitterly. An accident depended for interest on the vehicle you happened to be in at the time. 'I wasn't much hurt,' she added, but he was five years in the future, seeing his children, with a mother who let strangers give her lifts after knocking her off a push bike. But it had to be faced. 'Sandra, listen to me. This is a bad day. An unfortunate sort of thing to happen altogether, but we can all be reasonable, civilized, about it. Forget it, go on as we were. Can't we?'

She was silent so long that he took her by the upper arms, and shook her gently. 'Sandra! Are you listening to me?'

'Yes. I'm trying to think how we can do this. Tell me how. Have you announced the engagement to the press?'

'Nothing is going to happen until my parents return and re-open Byrne Place,' he said, in a reminding sort of voice. Of course, he had told her this before.

She nodded. 'But how will they do that? Credit, on the strength of your marriage to the dog biscuit fortune?'

He turned away, in distaste. 'Not worthy of you, Sandra. But you're hurt. I must be patient with you.'

'What will it be like in the future?' she persisted. 'You haven't said where we shall live, and what we shall do.'

'We shall live at Byrne Place, of course, and as to what we shall do, why, we shall behave like any other family in similar circumstances.'

'You mean I shall be groomed by your disapproving mother to help with her social occasions, and dress as she wants me to, and wait for you to come home at night. Or won't you do that?'

She was thinking of Audrey, and so was he, and he slowly went brick red, then whitened. 'I think I'd better come back at some other time when you've calmed down a bit,' he said.

'Yes, that's right, go and see Audrey. And in case she forgets to tell you, she's suggested that she comes to live with us, and help with … things. Her idea is that I shall have a lot of babies. That should keep me out of sight while you two enjoy life, shouldn't it?'

From the depths of her hurt and grief, she was being vulgar, she knew it. Stirring up a quarrel that would leave worse scars than even Audrey's had done. And then she saw something in Martin that she hadn't known was there. He was so angry at Audrey for making such a suggestion, that it showed in temper, in his eyes, his set white face, the tight lines around his mouth. He said nothing but turned to go out of the room, to Audrey, presumably, to take her up on that breach of everything he held precious.

She called him back. He stood for a moment, his back to her, presumably while he mastered his emotions, for when he turned, the signs of ill temper had gone. She was glad. That tiny crack in the curtain, showing such depth of fury, had frightened her. Not it alone, but the shock of realising that she honestly didn't know him, and if there was that much temper kept hidden and under control, there might be other things, too, that she wouldn't want to discover in his nature. He would be the father of her children…

'Yes, my dear?' he asked quietly enough.

'You can't just go like that, can you?' she said reasonably. 'I mean, we haven't resolved anything.'

'What is there to resolve? This is your birthday, and it's spoilt...'

'Yes, and Audrey told me what your present for me is,' she couldn't resist telling him, and waiting for the anger to flare again. But this time he kept a check on it, kept it hidden, behind the slight amused smile he had hastily pinned to his face.

'Never mind. I've got something else that she ... nobody knows about,' he said reassuringly. 'We'll go out to dinner tonight, just our two selves, and I'll give it to you then.'

'No, don't bother,' she said. 'Let's just say goodbye now. Oh, and telegraph your parents, or something, so they don't come back to Byrne Place for nothing.'

She thought, in her deep hurt, that the sight of the shock in him might assuage her own feelings, but it didn't. He couldn't have looked worse if she had struck him. 'You're not breaking it off?' he asked, his voice almost a croak. 'But you can't do that!'

'What's the matter? Don't you know any other unattached rich girls?' She hated herself for saying that, but she had to. She'd been so deeply hurt, she had to hurt back. And she had done. She'd frightened him, too.

She watched him struggle with himself. He really had iron resolution, she thought, in some admiration. 'I think you will think differently tomorrow,' he said. 'Please, Sandra, believe me – I didn't want you to find out about this. I didn't want you hurt. I can't be in love with you as I am with Audrey, but I like and respect you. My only regret was that you–'

'–were such a hoyden?'

'Well,' he said, with a touch of the old tender smile, 'I did call you that to your face. The only thing I ever did hold against you, and that surely could have been remedied. You won't racket around all your life, surely? You've got good bone structure and you're slim...'

'...and I could afford a good beauty parlour to make me over?' she retorted.

'Sandra, all I ever did to you was to fall for someone else, and when you fall in love, you'll know it's not a thing you can help. I wasn't going to do anything about it. I was going ahead with our marriage just the same. I would have been a good husband to you, even if I couldn't... Please believe me, and forgive me for something I couldn't do a thing about.'

Tears weren't far off. Painful, smarting tears. Sandra didn't cry easily. When she did, her face would be swollen and blotchy red and her eyes sore for days. She hated herself for not being able to make him love her as he had been able to love Audrey. She hated Fate for letting Audrey be the one to glow with a sensation Sandra had never felt. She cursed herself for a fool, not understanding that what she felt for this man was merely a juvenile crush she had mistaken for love. 'There's no need to talk about forgiveness. It's all over, forgotten. Cancel everything and forget you ever met me. You'll find another heiress, don't worry.'

'But you can't just blot out a thing like this, Sandra! Everything's gone too far – the Marriage Settlement, everything! Don't you understand?'

'My dear Martin, when you're as rich as we are, and only in trade, we have no finer feelings. I would have left you on the steps of the church, if I'd only discovered this then!' It wasn't true, but she drove herself to say it, for her one worry now was how her great-aunt would take all this. The old lady didn't like upsets, alterations in the process of the law. The summoning of the solicitors to cancel all this out might well make her unwell for days. But Sandra could do nothing about it.

'Very well,' Martin said, and looked at her.

'Don't you dare say you are sorry!' she gritted. 'I'll be all right. I'll meet someone who is a real person, not just someone who has to have my money to bale his family out!'

She caught her breath, guessing the retort she had left a way open for, wide open. But he didn't take the opportunity. He merely slightly bowed his head, and said, 'Very well. Goodbye, Sandra,' and went quietly out.

He had carried off the honours, she felt, the tears falling fast then. She turned to the window, her shoulders shaking, while she tried to stop crying. Somehow she had to get to her room, without any of the servants seeing her, so she must stop crying. She comforted herself by the thought that Martin hadn't said what she had feared he would say. It was left to Audrey to say that, later, much later, after Martin had gone. He had told Audrey Sandra had broken off the match.

She stormed into the room, and with none of Martin's care in avoiding a more unpleasant break between them, she exploded, 'That's right! Because he can't love you, you're going to ruin his family! You think someone else will come along, don't you? Well, he will, in droves. But you ask yourself, what he's wanting, the next man to get engaged to you! You, or all your filthy money! Because you'll never know, you know! You'll just never know!'

Great-Aunt Evadna would know what to do, Sandra told herself. But first she must examine her face and try to obliterate the ugly remains of her storm of weeping. There was some make-up left over, from the last time that Audrey had tried to change her cousin's face. Sandra put some on, but wasn't pleased with the effect, and washed it off again. What was the use of trying to make herself into something she was not?

She removed it, and fiercely combed her hair, and for once it lay down more or less tidy. She didn't stop to change her dress, and went in search of Miss Darley.

It wasn't until then that Sandra heard of her aunt's attack. She was horrified. 'When did it happen?' she gasped.

Her aunt's elderly maid looked accusingly at her. 'Hours ago, miss! And from what the poor lady said, when she was fetched in, it was your fault!'

'Mine! What a thing to say! I haven't seen her for hours! Too much has been happening to me today already! Goodness, the last time I saw my great-aunt was when she spoke to me after lunch.'

'Yes, and I left the poor lady peacefully sitting in the fountain garden. Are you sure you didn't go and upset her, miss?'

'You are not to talk to me like that!' Sandra stormed. 'No, I didn't go anywhere near her. I was in the music room with my cousin ... oh! Oh, no! No, it couldn't be! She couldn't have heard us having a row, not all that way away, could she?' but the maid's expression said that Miss Darley could and did.

'And now she's terribly ill?' Sandra whispered.

'Yes, miss. An attack, the doctor said. A nasty one. And she's got to be kept very quiet, and me, I will personally see she *is* kept quiet, miss, so you mark my words!'

It wasn't any use arguing with the woman. Miss Lake, as everyone called her, was a privileged servant. So far as Sandra knew, she had been with Miss Darley since they were both young. That was a long time, time in which a sort of friendship had sprung up between the two elderly women; a great friendship that was still tinged with deep respect on Miss Lake's part. She was proud to work for such a person. Miss Lake only, knew how near her mistress had come to marrying a title. She fiercely guarded her secret, and she fiercely guarded her mistress now, from this hoyden of a girl that, try as she would, Miss Lake couldn't bring herself to dislike.

Now Miss Audrey, the pretty one, there was a one she wouldn't trust any further than she could throw her, Miss Lake told herself, as she gently but firmly escorted Sandra to her part of the house. This one had a sensitive pair of eyes, when her guard was down. This was the one who would be loyal, Miss Lake felt, only the mistress couldn't see that. Funny, the way the mistress flayed herself over this one!

Sandra said, 'Well, when *can* I see her? I want to ask her advice!'

'Then you'll have a pretty good wait, miss, for your great-aunt is not to be asked for advice or anything else, for a long time, the doctor says.' She glanced at Sandra, thinking. There was a host of friends of the old lady's but none of them would be likely to appeal to this one, for advice giving. Miss

Lake said, 'Why don't you ask the doctor (when he comes back) for the advice your great-aunt was to give?' and Sandra nodded, much to her surprise. But Sandra wasn't even listening. She was thinking how odd it was that Aunt Evad. had to go and have a nasty turn, just when she wanted her to tell her what to do. Aunt Evadna had always prided herself on knowing just the right thing to do or to say. She had told Sandra severely that if you weren't gentry, then you had to learn a lot more about the ways of the world and how to meet them, and how to act.

She suddenly broke away, raced to her own room for a jacket, tore down the stairs and out. The maid shook her head, from the top of the stairs. How did that one think she would become the wife of that urbane young Martin Byrne, if she were going on like that? She half wondered whether the mistress would approve if she were to try and coach Sandra in time for her approaching engagement party. She decided against it in the end. First because she didn't like 'stepping out of her place', secondly because she had no means of knowing just what the mistress would think of such an idea, and thirdly because she hated to be made to feel a fool, which she surely would do if Sandra – as she had dreaded – would refuse to be coached for such a thing, and would make a great joke of her efforts, in front of everyone.

Well, at least the girl was going to have sense and wait for the arrival of the doctor, and put her problem to him. He was elderly, a very good type of man, who had known Sandra all her life. He would surely be the best one for confidences at a time like this!

She watched Sandra from the window, half running, half walking, down the drive, until she was out of sight, and then she turned back to her mistress, and forgot everything else. But when the doctor did arrive, he said he hadn't seen Sandra.

It wasn't likely that he had. Sandra, in her present mood, was ready to do anything that was *different*, however stupid. Somewhere inside her was a very sore place, but she wouldn't let herself think about it any more. Somehow she would have to get out of her system the thing she had called 'love', for want of a better word. Her whole existence had been geared to the thought that Martin Byrne would be in her life for ever, the closest person to her, the one on whom she could lavish the very deep well of affection she had to spill over. Now that was all gone, and a great empty sore spot remained, which must be obliterated and quickly. She hoped on one leg to kick a stone out of her shoe, and heard a car slow down so rapidly behind her that its brakes squealed. She turned casually to see if she knew the person. Most of her friends stopped their fast cars in such a cavalier fashion. It was no new thing.

This was not one of her friends. The young man got out of the car and stood looking at her, still hopping about wrestling with the stone. 'Want an arm to lean on?' he grinned, and she nodded, and put her hand on his arm, shook out the stone and replaced the shoe.

Sandra had never thought actively about how other people assessed the occupants of a house such as Darley House. She was used to living there, used to a large staff, and no money problems. Carelessly she accepted that, and never ever paused to consider whether new people she met had come from such a house, or a less large and prosperous one. People were people. She either liked them or she didn't, and mostly she did like them. She accepted them in good faith until one of them hurt her, and then she recoiled.

But by and large she was more interested in people than their background and connections. She would have been vastly surprised to know that this young man assessed her very quickly, by the dress she had bought off the peg, and decided she was one of the maids from the big house, out in her best for her day off. He said easily, 'Going to catch the bus? It's gone. Like a lift?'

The sort of thing he would have said to one of the maids but not to the great-niece of rich old Miss Darley. Sandra took his offer at its face value and got in. She never read newspapers, and wouldn't have feared abduction or any other crime, since she was well aware she looked and behaved like a hoyden, and was quite sure that such things only happened to the glamorous such as her cousin Audrey.

The young man said, 'I'm going into Huddlestone. Okay?'

'Why not?' Sandra said, getting in beside him. This, then, was what the maids talked about. A pick-up. Well, it seemed harmless enough, boring, too.

The young man registered that she wasn't carrying a handbag. Out for a pick-up, he thought; someone to pay for everything. He knew where he was now. 'What's the name?'

he asked easily.

Sandra frowned. 'You're giving me a lift. You don't want my history, surely?' so he laughed and said, 'Oh, I don't know. Names are useful as handles – I'm Bobby Anderson, and I'm a commercial traveller. Got good prospects.'

'Bully for you!' she said curtly. 'I'm Alexandra Josephine Stevens and I'm an heiress.'

To her surprise that made him laugh. 'I say, you did that jolly well! I like your style! Well, you can be Jo Stevens. How's that. As to the heiress bit, right then, you can pay your whack when we get to the hotel.'

He turned carefully from the side road into the mainstream. This car wasn't paid for yet, and he needed it for his work. Sandra said, 'Who said anything about a hotel? And I don't use cash. It gets charged everywhere, whatever I buy.'

It was the bitterness in her tones, as much as her careless manner, that made him stop laughing, and to think. Then it occurred to him that if she were a maid in the big house, she was probably throwing her weight about, pretending to be the boss's daughter, talking the toplofty way she did, whoever the heiress was. Certainly this girl didn't look like a rich kid, nor was she dressed like one. When the lights changed against him and he had to pull up, he glanced at her shoes. Shoes were a good thing to go by, but hers didn't help. She liked old shoes, but hand-made shoes never get too old to say what they are. But today she was wearing the cheap sandals she had bought to go with the dress. She now discovered they were making her feet ache. Nettled, she had to admit that the shoes that were made for her, felt better. But the man beside her priced her sandals and felt easier about her.

'I have to forget Martin and Audrey, and this way might be the way,' she told herself fiercely, and swallowed hard on the lump which wouldn't quite leave her throat since that distressing scene today.

She turned to the man beside her. 'Are you married?' she demanded.

'No, love,' he laughed. 'This is my first job. Give me a chance.'

'Right. Where are we going and what are we going to do?' she asked him.

Part of him wanted to believe that she was just a maid. Maids were fun; held down for most of the week, and wondering why on earth they had consented to take a live-in job, they were prepared to kick over the traces on their day off. Yet this girl didn't seem quite like that. She was more like a school girl, pretending to be grown-up, and not quite knowing what to expect, while trying to put on a bold face. He began to go off the idea. Something wasn't quite right.

'First, we'll pull up in some gateway and have a quiet talk,' he said.

'Well, we won't, you know!' she flashed. 'I've had enough talking for one day. You said Huddlestone. Let's go there and see what's going on!'

He laughed, and pulled in to the side of the road. 'Bossy little madam, aren't you,' he murmured and put an arm round her shoulders.

This was what she had wanted, to see how it would feel. To be able to tell herself that all she had felt for Martin was an illusion and better over and done with. If this stranger could make her feel the tremor of excitement that Martin had been able to call up, then she could slay Martin's image at a stroke. But it didn't. It made her feel so repelled, she wanted to hit him. She threw off his arm, and said, 'Cut it out! You offered a lift, and that was just what I wanted. If I wanted a petting party, it wouldn't be with … with any stranger. I've got enough friends in my own set for that purpose! And who do you think

I am, anyway? I told you my name and you'd better believe it's true!'

He tightened his hold on her. 'Baby, I like your style, like I said!'

She was overcome with revulsion. It was all her own fault. She had let herself in for this. It was true what Great-Aunt Evadna said. She was too careless. Didn't take the business of being an heiress seriously enough. It looked as if you couldn't have your cake and eat it – be a rich kid but fool around with the others just as if you were one of them. All of a sudden she disliked this man as much as she disliked herself. She slipped off her shoe. 'Just take your hands off me or I'll hit you,' she gritted.

'I'm not doing any harm! I just want a little talk! And anyway, where've you been all your life if you think you can cadge a lift and not play the rules as they're laid down?' He was hurt, and rather cross. She should have played it his way. Why make a fuss?

And then a car slid in beside them, a car she recognised. One of Audrey's friends, one who had been to Darley House in the past. Not a young man she cared about much, but at least she knew where she was with him.

'Having a rough house?' he asked, with

that humour she hadn't liked much in him. 'Can anyone join in?'

'Yes!' she said. 'I just wanted a lift!' She thrust away from the man beside her, picked up her shoe and limped out, to the other car. 'Benny, are you going anywhere special?'

'Get in and I'll take you back to the house. I wanted to see Audrey anyway,' the young man said easily. He pointedly ignored the commercial traveller, and roared his fast car away with an amused smile. 'Picking odd types to be pals with, aren't you, Sandra? What would Martin say?'

'Oh, plenty,' she agreed sourly, and almost disgraced herself at the thought of Martin's touch, Martin's distaste of such a thing as cadging a lift off a stranger. 'Going to tell him?'

'Shouldn't think so, not if you don't want me to. You two had a row?'

'You could say that!' she choked.

Benny took time to think. Tall, thin, casually good-looking, well-dressed as all their friends were, he hadn't a great fund of thought, though he was slick enough behind the wheel of his car. Finally he said, 'Want a bit of advice? Keep him away from Audrey. She forgets that things don't always belong to her.'

Sandra felt the choking sensation again. So everyone knew. They had known for some time, even Benny, who usually didn't look far below the surface of things. And she herself had been blind! Oh, what was the use? Might as well tell him and get it over!

'Too late,' she said. 'We're all washed up, Martin and me.'

Bobby was shocked at her tone and choice of words, as much as with the news. He swallowed, and said, 'Oh, that explains why my Mother's been searching for the announcement of the engagement. She thought perhaps they were waiting for his parents to come home.'

'That was the theory. Now leave me alone. If I'm bad company, pitch me out. I just wanted to get away from that oaf back there.'

'Yes, well, I wouldn't do that if I were you, not again, I really wouldn't,' Benny said earnestly. 'I mean, I might not be around to rescue you, might I?'

'Don't you start getting so matey!' she said savagely.

'What did I do?' he asked plaintively. He never managed to please anyone. His father had asked him caustically why he couldn't manage to interest the heiress, since quite clearly he wasn't going to be much good running the family firm in his father's footsteps. Being a solicitor took a certain amount of brains, his father told him sarcastically, and paused always, as if wondering how it was that his son had no brains and other men's sons had.

'Oh, I don't know. I'm just touchy. I thought you were being funny. Thanks for bailing me out without a scene. Trouble is with that sort of person, they won't take no for an answer. I think he thought I was a maid. I told him who I was–'

'Oh, I say, you never did!'

'Not right? Well, there you are! I never do anything right. But I've had a bit of a wallop below the belt today. Well, it's my birthday and I discovered Martin wanted me for my money, but he's in love with Audrey.' She swallowed hard. 'He still wants to marry me, mind you.'

Benny said, 'Oh, I say! Well, he would, I suppose. They really are on the rocks, and you will be rather rolling in the stuff, won't you?'

'You, too!' she said, her bitterness rising.

'Well, dash it, I don't see what you're making a big thing about it for. I mean to say, not many people fall in love, in spite of what you read. Seems to me if you can be sensible, and match the cash for a good family background, you're both home and dry, and might even like each other.'

'Thank you very much! If you want to know, I should want to be wanted for myself! Is that too much to ask?'

He pulled up at the traffic lights, and while waiting, considered it. He considered it for so long that Sandra glanced quickly at him. 'I'm not really with it, am I?' she asked quietly, and very seriously. 'I ought to know very well, that I'd only stand a chance of being liked for myself if I hadn't a bean. And do you know, I never thought of it before?'

Benny noticed the lights had changed, because people were blaring their horns at him. He hastily started up, jammed the gears, stalled the engine and collected a lot of abuse all round before he got away. 'Sorry about that,' he said. 'Fact is, I was a bit put out by your reasoning. I mean, you seem to care so much about it. I mean what does it matter, anyway?'

She sat very quietly, thinking about it. They had gone through the town, and out on to the motorway, before he realised he hadn't taken the turn for his home, where he had been going, and then he remembered he hadn't asked Sandra where she wanted to go. He had said he'd take her back to Darley House.

Sandra said, 'So if I asked you to marry me, it wouldn't be because you liked me if you said yes. It would be because you liked the idea of the fortune, wouldn't it?'

'Oh, I say!' he said, completely embarrassed. 'You shouldn't say things like that. I mean, you don't mean it, do you? You wouldn't want me. I mean, no family background to speak of, not like Byrne's, of course. Anyway, if he still wants to marry you, then that's still on, isn't it?'

'You mean, you'd be wanting my money, and not give a damn about me?' she persisted, and her heart cried out, because she remembered hearing one of the maids discussing this very thing, and at the time she thought it was the story of some film show the girl was recounting to her companion, as they cleaned the marble staircase of Darley House. A film! It was her, and her life story, they must have been discussing, and everybody, everybody in the world must know about it, and be thinking what a naive fool she must be! 'You make me sick!' she suddenly burst out, startling Benny so that he looked at her in astonishment. 'Look in front of you!' she screamed.

Benny liked speed. It never occurred to him to lower his speed when he was discussing something with a passenger. Sandra had thoroughly shaken him up with her argument and her unexpected bitterness, in such a usually cheerful girl. He couldn't cope, nor could he do much about the slower car which was leaving its lane to go into his. The two cars crashed, and like a slow motion picture, Sandra watched it all, and knew what was going to happen, even when the windscreen shattered and they dragged the other car with them into the central barrier...

Blacking out was the kindest thing that could have happened to her. She came to at intervals and was aware of noise and a lot of movement, and of being down low and people and vehicles up above her. Of Benny she could see and hear nothing, and she had no recollection of going in the ambulance to the hospital. Only movement, (which made pain) and inactivity, and she wanted to be out of it all, and away ... turn back the clock to this morning, before she had taken out her bike, and crashed into a man named Richard Norwood. That seemed a million years away, and she must be delirious, she told herself, for why would Richard Norwood be standing over her now?

The walls were white tiled, and there were one or two nurses, and the men all had white coats on, Richard Norwood too, which really didn't make sense, and it didn't make sense that he looked just like one would expect a doctor to look, and he seemed to fit in here, in this strange hospital, where everything had a special hospital smell, and people were behaving urgently, where she was concerned.

But why was Richard Norwood here, in a white coat? He should be at the Vicarage in Yelstone. She tried to speak, but he put a hand on hers, and said very quietly, 'Don't move. Don't worry. We'll have you comfortable very soon, Sandra.'

And one of the nurses said something to him, finishing by addressing him as 'Dr Norwood'.

THREE

In the past (when she had raced about, taking liberties on the main roads and thought it was a mark of getting old when people like her great-aunt warned her) she had seen accidents. A pile-up on the tricky roads near Brunchurch and Nosterwell, was no new thing. But now, in Nosterwell's District Hospital, a huge and impersonal building which reminded her of such things as Army barracks, prisons, workhouses, all the grimmest kinds of buildings she had ever read about but never seen, she reflected that she had never once given a thought to what was happening when the mess was cleared away and the motor road clean and normal again.

Somewhere people might be commenting on another careless driver, breaking the middle barrier and causing more hold-ups. But here, in this horrible place, there was plenty of evidence of what people outside never gave a thought to. She lay quietly when she came to, and gradually let the movements and significance of every living thing on the ward wash over her. She wondered about the appliances over every bed, for this was just an accident ward; gruesome things, she thought, until she realised there were even more gruesome additions to her own bed. It wasn't her way to call out and ask what happened to her. She lay like a wounded animal, quietly enduring, getting used to this new kind of existence, letting her chaotic pre-accident thoughts return to her in their own time.

Richard Norwood came and looked at her later. He studied her notes pinned to a board which he took off the end of her bed. She promised herself she would get at that board, as soon as she was allowed out to the bathroom, but when she tried to move, she saw in a blinding flash that that time would be so far ahead that it was useless to plan anything. She looked up at Richard Norwood and tried to think how it was she hadn't realised he was a doctor. She remembered all the allusions made to his skills, and recalled that she had quipped about his 'First Aid' – no wonder his aunt and uncle had looked a little odd. When they had given it up they must have thought she had known Richard for long enough to get to such joking terms with him, for surely he was too important here for a stranger to make jokes at his expense like that?

He said, with a quiet smile, 'So it's you again. Don't you know yet that when someone warns you to be careful, they mean it?'

'But it wasn't my fault,' she said faintly.

'Well, if it wasn't your fault that you were walking on the motorway and got mixed up with two mad drivers, I don't know what is. Don't you know you shouldn't walk on the motorway?'

She tried to think. How was it he didn't know she was a passenger? 'What happened to me?' she asked.

'Nobody seems to know. The two drivers didn't survive. You got mixed up with it somehow, and I can only think heaven was on your side. This is twice – don't let it be a third time, will you?'

'Superstitious?' she managed to quip.

He patted her shoulder, very gently, but even so, she winced. 'That's the girl! Take it in the right spirit. I'm afraid you'll be a bit sore all over for some time, but no internal injuries, thank heaven, and only one bone broken. Have patience. You'll soon be about,' he said quickly, not understanding her look of utter dismay. 'Oh, of course – a restless soul like you would take it badly. I forgot. Well, a rest won't hurt you,' and he turned away.

'Richard,' she said urgently. 'Oh, sorry, I suppose I should say "Doctor"', she added, as a passing nurse raised her eyebrows.

He smiled and came back. 'Richard will do. Sister knows we've met before. What can I do for you?'

'How did you get my name and … things, for the notes?' Only poor Benny could have supplied those.

'We had to go through the pockets of your coat. There was a letter addressed to you – at 17 Duke Street, Brunchurch. That's right, isn't it?'

Her heart turned over. So he didn't know she was Sandra Stevens of Darley House! For some reason she was glad, absurdly glad. She couldn't bear it if he found out, too, that she was an heiress. His was a friendship she wanted to be sure she had earned, by herself alone. The fact that she hadn't had her handbag, and that Benny had not been in a position to identify her, filled her with such relief that she closed her eyes so this nice young doctor shouldn't see. For answer, she said, 'What a lot you are, going through a person's pockets. You didn't let anyone read that letter, did you?'

'No. Not necessary since the address was outside. But we couldn't get any answer when the police went there. Where would your aunt be?'

'She's somewhere else and I don't want her to know yet,' Sandra said quickly. Police, going to the house? Oh, that was what they did when there was no telephone, she supposed. She passionately didn't want her great-aunt to know about this, not after the attack she had had. 'Look, tell them to leave it to me,' and her voice sounded infinitely tired. 'I want to write and tell her what happened. In my own way, so it isn't a shock. She isn't expecting me back yet.'

'On your way to inflict your disrupting personality on some unfortunate friends, I suppose,' he said gently, laughter in his voice.

'That's right,' she said gratefully, and managed a smile.

'Well, when you feel able, dictate your letter to a nurse, and we'll get it taken to your home,' and he again patted her shoulder.

'No. Must write it myself,' she gasped, but he shook his head, his smile fading, and his glance took in both her hands. She lifted one an inch or two, with difficulty. 'What's the matter with them?' she cried. It was the first time she had noticed the heavy bandaging.

'I told you, you took a bashing. But don't worry, it all looks worse at first than it really is.'

After he had gone, she lay there thinking. Impatiently shaking off the fluffiness of her thinking processes, willing herself out of the clouds of semi-consciousness that she supposed was the aftermath of coming round. How she wanted to drift off to sleep and forget everything, but she dare not – not till she had done something about explaining her absence from Darley House, in such a way as to foil these people at the hospital from knowing who she was. It explained, she supposed, why she was on an open ward and not in a private room. Great Aunt Evadna always had a private room in hospital. Sandra shivered at the thought of such isolation.

She also shivered at the way Fate worked. To think that that old letter should be in her coat pocket, all that time, with Melchett's address on it. Mrs Melchett had been a maid at Darley House, one of the few who looked on Sandra's escapades with kindliness, and when Melchett left and got a cottage in

Brunchurch, her sister, later housekeeper at Darley House, was grateful that her only relative lived so near. She sometime let Sandra take things over to her sister, who was so much older than she was, and not so active. There had been a bit of a conspiracy about getting a present for Melchett from a postal shopping firm. The housekeeper was old-fashioned, but Sandra said she would do it, and arranged to have it sent to the Duke Street cottage in her name. She couldn't remember at this stage what had happened about the gift, but Melchett was rather odd about the correspondence being sent to her. 'I don't mind, miss. In fact, I was half wondering if I'd suggest you having your mail sent here – private mail, that is, the sort you didn't want steamed open first. It'd be safe with me, you know that.' And that was the first time the startled Sandra realised that Audrey opened her mail. Why, for letters from Martin?

Lying there, she had the time and opportunity to think over a lot of things she had been too careless (or trusting) to notice. Melchett had also delicately suggested that Audrey ran up bills in Sandra's name, which explained the mystery of her great-aunt's remark that she didn't mind Sandra throwing money about, if only she looked any better for it.

And now she was going to ask Melchett to do something for her again. 'Dear Melchett, Will you let my aunt think I am still with my friends, until she is better? The fact is, I got a lift from someone, who had a bit of an accident. Nothing to worry about. I'm in Nosterwell & District Hospital, and I don't want any visitors until I've got rid of some bandaging. I know you'll understand,' she dictated to the nurse, and finished, 'Just sign it "Sandra", will you?'

'Who is Melchett? Your aunt's friend?' the nurse asked, and Sandra said fervently, if not with strict truth, 'Very much so.'

'Well, it's decent of you not to let your aunt know, but won't someone else leak the news to her? You will get visitors, you know, in spite of this noble effort. A lift, you say?'

'No, no, that's not true, but I don't want Melchett to come over and want police enquiries and everything. I don't know what happened – I wasn't paying attention–' How many lies could you tell, to keep out of the limelight, in order to keep a friend?

They would come, of course – Audrey and Martin, the solicitor, the local doctor. The press would get to hear of it through them, and she would watch her one bid for anonymity fade, losing Richard Norwood's friendship, she told herself bitterly.

But they didn't come. Melchett was too sincere in carrying out Sandra's wishes, to allow the secret to leak out. The housekeeper kept it, too, and told everyone she had heard in a casual way from Sandra that she was staying with friends – a thing which didn't send Sandra's stock up, with anyone, least of all with Martin. And Evadna Darley lay fretting because she, too, had told nobody what she had heard in the garden, and which she was sure, was more than enough to send a high-spirited girl like Sandra, off on her own, to brood over a future that she now knew the truth about, but could see no way of changing.

Benny's funeral was a big affair, and the father who had been so impatient with his son's inability either to become a good solicitor or find an heiress willing to marry him, was reputed to say that someone had cut short a most promising young life. Sandra read the account in the newspapers, when her bandages had been taken from her hands, and she marvelled that nobody could have seen her, and what had really happened to her. But it had been her fault, and she shrugged it off. What hurt her most was that neither Melchett nor the housekeeper had bothered to write to her. She missed the point that she hadn't been able to tell them she had used her own name, and that nobody connected it with Darley House.

Inexpressibly bored with the inactivity, she started to help the young nurses who changed her bandages and asked a lot of questions about what they did. Hospital life began to intrigue her.

One day Richard Norwood discovered that she had no visitors, so he slipped into the habit of spending an hour or two with her when he could. And his aunt and uncle, at his request, came, too.

But this was dangerous from Sandra's point of view. Now it was a completely fanatical desire on her part to keep her identity secret. It made, at times, a useful game, keeping alert so that she should not be guilty of telling a direct lie, but at the same time becoming expert at evading the direct questions kindly people put to her. She could say, of course, that she had no parents, and this was true. But she couldn't say why she had no job, which bothered Richard's aunt and uncle. For such a nice girl to make no attempt at earning some sort of a living to recompense an aunt who had such small means that she lived in a cottage in Brunchurch's Duke Street, was hard for them to understand. Nor could Sandra say ill health prevented her from working, for her own blazing good constitution was the one thing that had got her through the injuries she had received – injuries that Richard Norwood had, needless to say, played down a great deal. How much he had played them down, only time allowed her to discover.

'Why didn't you tell me the truth?' she demanded one day, when other people had visitors, and neither his aunt nor his uncle had been able to come.

'I had my reasons,' he said quietly. 'The same as you no doubt have your reasons for shutting me out when I want to swap confidences.'

She looked up quickly. 'You mean about the accident?'

'Not necessarily, though sometimes I think you know perfectly well what happened, and that it wasn't conceivable that you could have been walking on the motorway – nor cycling, for that matter. I suppose you were in one of the cars, and were thrown out.'

'Well, it doesn't matter now, does it? I

hope to be out of here soon.'

'Back to the job you had, or has that folded up?' he asked.

She was puzzled, genuinely puzzled. He could see that. So he said, 'Look, Sandra, you might say it's none of my business, but I want it to be!'

'Because you're my friend?' It was the one thing that mattered in all the world.

'You could say that,' he agreed, hesitating. To be just her friend was not what he wanted at all. 'Why don't you trust me with the truth? Or is it that you want me to guess?'

'Okay,' she said easily, her mind half on the problem of why Audrey hadn't made some attempt to find her, and how she could discover what her great-aunt's state of health was. She had a newspaper on the side of the bed, that she had folded ready to read when Richard had come. 'You guess.'

'Well, I would guess that you were having a lift in the boss's car. Why not? A secretary gets taken home when she's been working late. Only it wasn't late that day, was it, and you were probably worried that his wife would wonder at the unusual time. Tell me, Sandra,' he probed, anxious for her peace of mind as much as anything.

But she couldn't give her complete attention to him. In the announcement of forth-coming marriages, she had seen Audrey's to Martin. 'Sandra, am I right?' Richard pressed. 'I'm not saying you were doing anything wrong, but it can't be comfortable for a wife to–'

'Benny wasn't married,' she said carelessly, grappling with this new piece of news. What was her great-aunt doing, to let this happen? Or had not her great-aunt recovered. She grasped her middle, taking the blow of that thought, there. Richard said, 'What did you say?'

She shook her head, unwilling to answer.

'What is it? What have you seen in that paper?' Richard asked.

She looked at him, appalled. The shock of that news was one thing, but how could she have been so stupid as to think she could keep anything secret from him for long? The district wasn't all that scattered. She couldn't imagine how it was that someone hadn't recognised her already. She supposed, with a sinking heart, that people saw what they expected to see, and who would expect to see old Miss Darley's heiress in an open ward, her hair like a scarecrow's since she hadn't troubled to have it decently styled for ages, and nobody from the big house visiting her?

Richard said again, 'Sandra!' but she was saved from having to answer him as someone came to fetch him down to Casualty. She breathed again. She didn't want him to find out who she was, and above all, since it had gone on for some days, she didn't want him to know she hadn't been straight with him. It wasn't what she had wanted at all.

And then she pushed that aspect to the back of her mind and considered the announcement that had made her almost betray herself. Martin and Audrey.

She closed her eyes, but the tears pushed their way under her lids, and ran scalding down the sides of her face to the pillow. What else had she expected? She knew those two were in love. But how come Martin hadn't troubled to find the girl he was supposed to be engaged to, the girl with all the money coming to her? Her heart did an uneasy skid from sheer upset, as she faced the truth. Probably her great-aunt was angry with her being away so long without a word and had made Audrey her heiress after all? That her great-aunt hadn't survived her attack that day, was a thing Sandra wouldn't let herself think about. In her way, she was fond of Miss Darley, and trusted her.

And then another shock was in store for her. Not then, but later, when everyone else was having visitors, and Richard appeared. She caught her breath for now surely he would demand an answer to his question.

He certainly came purposefully towards her bed, but he was smiling broadly, and so was the nurse who walked smartly beside him.

'Well, Sandra, I've had my place usurped at your side this visiting hour, would you believe it?' he said in his warm friendly voice.

The nurse said, 'Don't look so miserable, my dear. Dr Norwood is as pleased as I am that you've got a real visitor of your own, for once. Shall I fetch her in?'

'Her?' Sandra licked her lips. Surely, surely it wouldn't be Audrey, come to see her after becoming officially engaged to Martin? Surely not? 'Who is it?' she forced herself to ask.

The reply was just as much of a shock to Sandra, though it didn't appear to be Audrey. 'Well, my goodness, there was enough song and dance about that letter you wrote to her. It's your aunt, of course!'

FOUR

That day a new intake had arrived in the bed on Sandra's left. Another accident case, and she hadn't been to theatre, but had had her fractures encased in plaster, and seemed to find the ward and its busy life a new and exciting existence for her. She talked non-stop; a little woman with greying hair who Sandra felt she vaguely recognised, although her name – Franey – meant little. But surely Mrs Franey would start asking questions soon of Sandra. She had already rolled her head round inquisitively and smiled invitingly until Sandra had closed her eyes. Mrs Franey had listened unashamedly to Sandra's conversation with Richard Norwood, and had no doubt seen Sandra trying to keep back the tears, and wanted badly to know what was in the newspaper, but Sandra had given it to one of the younger nurses to take away and read over her coffee break.

And now Mrs Franey wanted to hear all about Dr Norwood visiting the patient beside her, and about the surprise visitor, although she herself had two women by her bedside.

'My aunt?' Sandra licked her lips again, and tried to think. How *could* it be Miss Darley? Why *should* it be? If she had found out Sandra was on an open ward, she would have had her moved to a side ward before she had appeared in person. 'Did she say so?' she asked idiotically, she felt.

The nurse laughed. 'Goodness, won't you let her come in? Such a sweet little old lady, and as if I wouldn't know she was your aunt – she asked most severely to be taken to see Miss Stevens, so I knew at once who she was!'

Sandra felt a little less shaken. That wasn't Miss Darley's entrance! Not like her at all. She watched the nurse go smartly out to fetch in the visitor. Richard said, bending over her, 'I'm very glad. I wanted you to see someone belonging to you!' and no doubt he was going to stay and meet the relative. And there she was, a neat, respectable, dumpy little figure in her Sunday clothes, her brimmed felt hat trimmed with a new ribbon bow, and a new hat pin jamming the whole structure firmly on to her head. Somewhere under that preposterous hat was the bun that had always neatly terminated her greying hair, and on her lined face was the same faintly disapproving air that had always been there.

Sandra meant every word when she said, 'Oh, you've come – you've found where I am! I am so glad!' She couldn't hold out her arms – everything was still bandaged. Melchett clucked severely (hadn't she always, when Sandra had behaved disgracefully?) and she said, with truth, 'Dear life, look at you! I always knew something dreadful would happen to you one day!' and although she had managed to leave off the habitual 'miss' in among all that, it was very much the usual thing Melchett would have said to Sandra, in similar circumstances, when she had been in service at Darley House.

Richard pulled out the stool for her, and Sandra held her breath, in case Melchett should say 'Thank you, sir!' but the poor woman seemed incapable of taking anything in properly. She nodded and sat down, and hardly seemed to hear Richard's remark, 'I am very glad to meet Sandra's aunt at last!'

Melchett said earnestly to Sandra, 'What happened – just tell me that! I don't know how I shall sleep tonight for thinking of the sight of you, I do not, and that's a fact!'

Richard gave a kindly, half amused smile, put up a hand in farewell to Sandra, and walked quickly away, happy that Sandra was settled with such a devoted old relative. Sandra stared at Melchett in utter dismay.

'Come closer,' she whispered, unhappily conscious of Mrs Franey trying to lean over to hear what was going on, in spite of her visitors being still there.

Melchett obliged, and whispered, 'Miss, what shall I do? Look what you've landed me into! Acting the lie, that's what I am! But I knew what you meant in your letter. I knew you were in some trouble. Oh, dear, am I doing the right thing, I wonder?'

'Yes, you are! You are good and faithful – too good to me! You always have been! I knew I could trust you. I couldn't think who else to write to. You won't let me down, will you?'

'No, miss,' Melchett whispered unhappily, 'But my sister is so cross with me. Says I'm not doing the right thing, no matter which way you look at it. Well, I had to tell her, didn't I? Because how else was your aunt to know?'

'I didn't want her to. It was only face-saving – I mean, you were supposed to be my aunt,' Sandra whispered. 'I was dictating the letter to a nurse – well, look at my hands – so they all knew what was in it. You do understand, don't you?'

'No, miss. I only understand you've been up to something again and this time you're properly in the soup if I may say so,' Melchett said, and although she was still whispering, the severity of her tones got through to Sandra, who wondered how much longer she could rely on Melchett's secrecy.

'Well, you must know what's going on,' Sandra said crossly. 'You must have known all the time. I only saw the announcement in the paper today.'

'Oh, yes, Mr Martin,' Melchett said, nodding and looking down at her work-worn hands, as if for inspiration. 'Well, I don't suppose it was any more surprise to you, miss, than it was to all of us. Seen it coming for a long time, we have. But somehow we didn't think you'd mind.'

'Melchett, you haven't said how my aunt is.'

Melchett thought Sandra meant how she had taken the business of the engagement to Audrey. 'Seems like she intended it to happen, or at least didn't mind, though what's going on in that quarter, I can't think.'

'But Martin has to marry money,' Sandra

92

said feverishly. 'How will he manage? My cousin Audrey hasn't got any.'

'She's got prospects,' Melchett said hardily. She wasn't one to scheme or intrigue. Everyone else knew about this so she didn't see why Sandra shouldn't. Sandra had always been a favourite of Melchett's, over the years, because Sandra had been the honest one, the one who got into hot water but took it with courage when it came to owning up and punishment. Audrey wriggled out of trouble, or laid the blame neatly on other people. Audrey was not her favourite. But now things had changed a little. Melchett didn't like all this intriguing on Sandra's part. She didn't know what the accident meant, or how it had come about. But she did know other things, things she couldn't forgive Sandra for. She said so now.

'I don't know what this is all about or how you got into this state but I do know that that dear lady got her bad turn because she heard what was going on that day. You and Miss Audrey quarrelling like that. And then when she was a bit better and asked for you you never came. So she thought she hadn't laid her love in the right place all these years, and she altered her Will. And that's about the beginning and end of it, miss.'

Mrs Franey's visitors were garrulously telling her about another piece of scandal locally, so she could no longer listen in, for which Sandra was very glad, but it made little difference in the end. This piece of news was shattering. Not the fact that she had lost the money but the fact that her great-aunt, the one she had always trusted in, had turned against her and accepted Audrey.

'What have you got to say to that, miss?'

'Nothing much. I suppose she didn't know where to find me. I was in here. I got mixed up with a car crash. I couldn't come and see her, could I? Doesn't matter, though. I'll see her when I get about again.'

'No, you won't, miss,' Melchett said. 'She won't be here. She's going on a cruise with Miss Lake, to recover her health, just as soon as she gets over this little lot.'

'Oh, I wish I could use my hands. I could write her a letter, explaining, and you could give it to her.'

'Not me, miss. Not even Miss Lake would help you now, and she's always been the one to dote on you, in secret, as you might say. But they all took it so badly, that there was no word from you and that poor lady calling for you.'

'I couldn't come. I told you why!'

'Makes no difference, miss. You must have been in trouble as usual to get in this state. In somebody's car, was it?'

'Someone I knew, he gave me a lift. It wasn't my fault that he wasn't paying attention to his driving. I've got nothing against him, but I just won't be blamed for his not surviving. And that's the reason I didn't go back home.'

'Well, I'm sorry, I really am, but there it is.' She began to gather her things, then paused. 'Oh, well, it's many a year since I first got you out of your big scrape and presented you in decent condition to the drawing-room,' and an unwilling smile fleeting over her face briefly softened it. 'You can't help being what you are, I suppose, and I can't help being what I am, and I can't go home and try to sleep tonight for wondering what will become of you now. See, the house will be shut up. What will become of you?'

Sandra stared at the ceiling. Such a little while ago, the world was her oyster and she didn't appreciate it. Words came tumbling from her lips, words that nobody would have expected the happy-go-lucky Sandra to use. 'It depends on how I shall be, but they tell me I'm strong and young and will mend. So I shall get a job. Train for some-thing.'

'*You*, miss?' Melchett was almost but not quite amused.

'Yes, Melchett, I shall stand on my own two feet, and,' she said fiercely turning round to stare into the lined face of a trusted friend, 'I shall know who my friends are, because I shall be just me, hard-up and not asking any quarter of anyone, and not there for the Martins of this world to–' and then she turned away, sharply, and bit hard on her bottom lip.

'Yes, I know,' Mrs Melchett said, very gently. 'Fair doted on that one, you did – I know. We all knew. I can't think why Miss Darley didn't ... oh, well, it's none of my business, I suppose. She was hurt, too. Give her time, miss, and she may change things–'

'She can't, not any more. Audrey will marry Martin, on the assumption that – well, the Marriage Settlement will be set – no, things can't be undone this time.'

Melchett shook her head, wondering at the doings of the people above stairs and how it was that they never seemed to act in the sensible way that people below stairs had always seemed to do. She was a product of the years of her youth. She couldn't move with the times. Useless for the Darley House housekeeper to tell her that one day the house would be closed up, the staff dispersed and she herself would be unlikely to get that sort of job anywhere else. Melchett felt it was a great shame that things could change, so that people like this girl had been tearing about like a hooligan instead of having some sense knocked into her. Why had Sandra behaved like a hoyden, Mrs Melchett asked herself in utter bewilderment? She was a nice girl. Anyone could see that – even if they hadn't know her all her life as Melchett had. And now what was there for her? Marriage to someone who was hard-up and of no count?

'Don't leap into more trouble, miss,' she whispered urgently.

Richard came on to the ward again, this time with a great sheaf of roses and a huge basket of fruit. Some of the visitors saw them and gave a gasp of pleasure. Not many such things were seen on this ward. They watched to see where they would go. He came over to Sandra's bed.

'I was walking down to Casualty and minding my own business when a most glamorous young woman thrust these at me and said they were for you. You never told me you had someone who would make you presents like these, Sandra!'

'It wouldn't have been true,' Sandra said. 'I haven't such a person,' and she turned the card over with difficulty to read what it said.

It was in Martin's handwriting. 'Only just heard about you – didn't know you knew poor old Benny that well! Anyway, get better quickly.'

How in the world had Martin come to hear of that? How could he know? It might well mean that everyone would soon know. She shivered a little, at the way he had reacted to the news. Of course, it would make him feel less bad about everything, if he could be sure that she had been with Benny at the time of his accident.

She said, 'Put them on the centre table, for the rest of the patients. I don't care for fruit or roses,' and she quietly tore the card into shreds.

Melchett got up, embarrassed, and glanced at Richard, who was also looking rather odd. 'Yes, well, I'll go now. I'll come again as soon as I can,' and said 'miss' with a movement of her mouth only. She couldn't not say it but she had remembered not to utter it aloud. Sandra nodded at her, and blew her a kiss – a kiss she really meant. Melchett's lips trembled, she nodded and turned away, and then the visitor's bell went, to clear the wards.

As she went past Mrs Franey's bed, the woman couldn't resist leaning over and saying, 'Why, Mrs Melchett! I couldn't help hearing them say you were this young lady's aunt. I didn't know you *had* a niece her age!'

Sandra had never seen Melchett look so fierce. She turned on Mrs Franey and said with ferocity, 'Well, how should you? You don't know anything about me so be good enough to mind your own business, Winnie Franey!' And she stomped out of the ward, and got lost in the press of other visitors.

'Well!' Mrs Franey said, as her own visitors took their leave. 'I only asked kindly. After all, she's a regular customer of mine!'

Customer. Oh, heavens, Sandra thought. That's where I know her from. The second grocer's in the High Street in Brunchurch. It would be all over the place in no time.

Raggedly, the visitors left. Not nearly such a nice scene as the visitors coming, Sandra thought, through swimming eyes. Richard had in bewilderment, done as she had asked. Why? No argument about such a bad-tempered act. Perhaps he could see how upset she was over something. Would he come back to ask about it? She hoped he wouldn't, but it wasn't likely that he would let things rest.

She thought about it. Today had been eventful in news. Audrey engaged to Martin. Martin finding out she had been Benny's passenger, and hiding behind that knowledge. Audrey herself coming in with those gifts, which might possibly have indicated that they were her choice, her idea. Sandra could just imagine her, now the money was hers. Audrey's ... and not Sandra's any more.

Suddenly it was as if a weight had rolled off her. Now she was free! She could do anything she liked when she got out of here! Anything! And she could trust people to like her for herself!

'I say! I say, dear, I never meant any harm,' Mrs Franey was calling to her. 'Only, that nice young doctor being at your bedside and all ... well, it wasn't likely that you'd belong to Mrs Melchett. Well, everybody knows she used to be a maid up at the big house. Well, I mean...'

Sandra kept her eyes shut.

'Well, I must say, it isn't every girl who has a handsome young doctor flitting round her like that! Been in and out several times to see you today, since I came in, hasn't he?'

Sandra turned and said blightingly, 'He happens to be related to the vicar. That's all, positively all. And I don't want to talk, thank you.'

Mrs Franey said, imperturbably, 'Oh, that's just what they all say, dear, when they don't want to admit a chap's sweet on them,' so Sandra hunched her shoulder till the pillow stuck in her ear one side and she pulled the blanket somehow up above the other ear.

Think, she told herself. Think. Never mind that woman's voice. It will go on and on. She can't help herself. Just shut it out by thinking. Plenty to think about. Not Martin, nor Audrey – forget those. Think about yourself, what you'll do...

Darley House would be closed. She thought about that. She had only seen it closed once. It became a mausoleum, with cold cotton covers over everything, and the doors locked, one by one, and the windows shuttered against intruders. All the small things, the rare porcelain and glass, the pictures, put away in packing, hidden from the light, until the house was opened again. Only one servant left there, to act as caretaker. Everything silent, cold, unwelcoming. No longer her home.

Her heart started to bang wildly. Why hadn't Great-Aunt Evadna written to her? Perhaps she had, and left it with the solicitors, until Sandra had been traced. Sandra shrank from communicating with the solicitors. The fortune her aunt possessed was hers to do as she liked with, but the way she had disposed of it now, hurt so very much. She might have given Sandra chance to explain, might have waited until she had found Sandra, before acting so precipitately. Well, she had railed against so much money, Sandra reminded herself, and now she had got her wish and she was free. Free to be on her own, support herself. But how? She wasn't trained for anything. What was there she could do except work behind a shop counter, and who would want her, for everyone would know who she was.

The nurse came over. 'Wakey-wakey!' she said in a jocular voice that made Sandra even more depressed. 'The surgeons say you are to start moving, young lady, so come tomorrow, out of bed you get, while it's made. And the next day you can help us to make it. Help us, yes, that's an idea. Too much of this slacking.'

This nurse was famous for telling those who were incapable of movement that they were slacking, but it sowed the seed of an idea in Sandra's unhappy heart.

It was inevitable that the news should leak out to the press. It was a quiet period. A reporter came to see Sandra. The ward was a-buzz with excitement, so she told him loud and clear, uncaring who heard, that she had displeased her aunt, and was no longer the heiress, and that if he wanted a story, he'd better go and interview her cousin Audrey, who liked publicity.

Audrey could have told Sandra that it wasn't good policy to upset the press, even the local boys. She was given a most un-favourable small spot in the paper, and someone managed to send a cutting to Miss Darley. The solicitors were also informed about it, and when Sandra applied to them for permission to join the staff of the hospital as a nurse, it wasn't denied. Miss Darley, they wrote to tell her, no longer had any interest in Sandra's affairs. She could please herself.

She asked to be moved to another part of the ward, because of the volubility of her neighbour. Sandra's bed couldn't be moved, but Mrs Franey's could, and was. The busy little woman took the greatest umbrage to being moved, and Sandra could hear her, bitterly talking about her, six beds further down the ward. And Richard didn't come near her.

That, perhaps, was the bitterest blow of all. Later that day she was moved to another ward, a small one with two other beds, both empty.

'What's this for?' she asked fiercely, but the nurse merely smiled.

Later the ward sister explained. 'You are having visitors this afternoon. Naughty girl, you didn't tell us who you really were!'

Sandra's heart sank. Visitors. Audrey and Martin. Who else? And Audrey would be arranging for this. 'I wanted to stay on the ward,' she said angrily, but the ward sister's brows shot up. She had already had a run-down on Melchett's visit, who Melchett was, according to Mrs Franey, and what had happened when the reporter had come. Flowers came by the dozen, from friends of Miss Darley's, and the bewildered Sandra began to feel that perhaps the mercurial Miss Darley had changed her mind. And then Audrey appeared.

Audrey paused in the doorway and looked at the attachments to Sandra's bed and limbs. 'What happened to you?' she breathed.

She drifted over, and a hovering young nurse pulled out a chair for her and was rewarded by Audrey's best smile. Audrey looked good and smelt good. Sandra, angrily trying to decide which question she wanted to ask first, noticed that Audrey, with a great lack of taste, was wearing the Darley emeralds. 'Only the paste set,' she murmured, following Sandra's glance. 'Must make Aunt Evadna happy, seeing her favourite gems courting the daylight.'

'How is she liking the Greek islands?' Sandra forced herself to ask.

Audrey shrugged. 'I wouldn't know. Are you comfortable? Anything you want?'

'Yes. To have the answers to a lot of questions. No, don't get up. They don't concern you being made the heiress. That never bothered me. What I want to know is, how come people knew who I was, and that I was with poor Benny at the time of the crash?'

Audrey looked amused. 'There couldn't be two scruffy individuals like you. Someone in a passing car recognised you, of course.'

'And did they tell Aunt Evad at once?' That was really all Sandra wanted to know. Had she contributed to a further shock for her aunt? Audrey said, 'I haven't a clue. They said she was too ill to see me so I suppose she wasn't allowed newspapers or letters. I've been away.'

'Where?' Sandra demanded, trying to piece it all together. Had Audrey gone away before their aunt got dangerously ill? Was she staying with Martin's family? Well, of course she would be!

Audrey smiled faintly. 'I was staying with the Egger family. You didn't like them. Odd, that. They're friends of Martin's people.'

And lived near them. All very convenient. Sandra said, 'So now you have all the money–'

'Correction. I am named as our dear aunt's heiress, so that makes it all right with Martin's people.'

'But how does it, if you haven't got your hands on the money, to bale them out?'

'You never had a clue, did you?' Audrey asked wearily. 'The fact that we're engaged to be married, is enough to float them,' and she took off her glove and showed her engagement ring. The one Sandra had known would be used; the one she herself didn't want. On Audrey, it looked right, somehow. She smiled, brilliantly, at Audrey. 'I wish you luck,' she said, and she meant it. The only hurt she had now was that Miss Darley no longer seemed to be fond of her. That was a very real loss.

Audrey was put out. She blinked, as she said, 'What about Martin? Aren't you furious, him ditching you for me?' but Sandra shook her head.

'Then there's someone else! Who? Well, you can't keep it to yourself – we're big news! You know that. Locally, anyway. And Great-Aunt Evadna ought to be told.'

'Why? She doesn't want to know about me any more.'

'Don't be stupid.' Now the smiling mask had slipped and Audrey looked at Sandra with the old veiled animosity. 'She got ill again when some clot told her about you being in an accident with Benny. She never did like Benny.'

'So she didn't go away to the Greek islands at all!'

'Did I say she did?' Audrey got up. 'The thing is, are you going to see Martin? He's waiting downstairs.'

'What do I want to see Martin for?' Sandra said fiercely. 'And who arranged all this? I was all right on the open ward. Anyway, I'm going to train as a nurse when I'm about again–'

'Heavens, our dear great-aunt won't like that.'

'She won't care. The solicitors said so. I've written to them. And no, I don't want to see Martin.'

But he was there, in the open doorway, armed with tea roses. He looked much the same as on that other occasion when he had come in suddenly and admitted that he cared for Audrey.

Sandra tried to think what could have happened in their proper sequence of events. Their aunt had heard them quarrelling and had collapsed – she herself had gone out and got involved with Benny's accident and had been brought to this hospital – finally Melchett had contacted her, and told her that Miss Darley had made Audrey the heiress, and she was to marry Martin. Sandra looked at him with no great liking, and said, 'You'd better come in and shut the door, now you're here.'

'Good heavens, girl, what happened to you,' he said easily, bending over her, depositing the flowers, a huge box of chocolates, and glossy magazines in one practised swoop, as he kissed her forehead and smiled down at her. Richard, from the still open doorway, looked quietly on. Nobody noticed him. Sandra's eyes were blinded by angry tears, and she couldn't speak, so it was Martin who did the talking. 'I expect the house will be opened up again, as your aunt didn't go away after all, so do pack up this futile idea of being a nurse – I don't suppose you'll be on your legs for that number of hours for ages. Come home, do, and be taken care of decently, there's a love.' Incredible how much practised tenderness Martin could manage to infuse in his voice. Richard walked quietly away.

She had seemed so much a part of their lives, he reflected, and yet why should he mind? He worked it out. Her aunt was on the staff of Darley House, and she would have been brought up there, of course. And that good-looking type would have seen as much of her as the glamorous niece of the rich old party who owned Darley House. Audrey... Richard reflected that there wasn't another name that would suit that girl as much. Brought up in the lap of luxury, and Sandra saw it from a distance, and was probably quite overcome with that fellow being kind to her.

He thought of that tiresome woman, Mrs Franey, and of the way she had gossiped on the ward. He had come across the newspaper they had all been avidly reading and talking about, but it merely tied in with his own private thoughts, and he couldn't understand why they should all be so scandalised. He had cut out the small piece and kept it, read it over and over again, until he knew it by heart: 'Guess who has come a real cropper this time? Some young women cultivate the rich and elderly by making themselves attractive and pleasant. Others just set out to attract attention by becoming notorious. But what, we ask ourselves, does a well-known rich old resident see in a certain young woman who would look more at home in the back streets of Brunchurch than the marble halls of the well-known mansion on the hill above our town? Trussed up in the Accident Wing, she is out of action for quite a while, but one feels sorry for her poor old auntie – to say nothing of the young man who kindly gave her a lift and finished up in Nosterwell's District Hospital Morgue.'

The gossip columnist of the local newspaper was no kinder than the next man, but Sandra had angered him. He was safe because he hadn't mentioned her name. But everyone knew the significance of it, except Richard, who still naturally believed her old auntie was the servant who had visited her in hospital. He was furious on Sandra's behalf but longed to be able to talk to her about it, and couldn't. She had kept him at arm's length.

He hadn't a lot of time to give to thinking about it. There were other things on his mind. He had been called home because of Philippa.

There was a problem! Most of his spare time he had was given to study. There was little spare cash in his family. His widower father, the local G.P. in a village that was painfully growing to the size of a small town, without the trade to boost it, had little money enough for his own needs. He had to employ a housekeeper. Philippa, a distant relative with no home of her own, had seemed the ideal choice. She was devoted to his father, although she was only Richard's age. Sometimes he wished that his father would marry Philippa. That would solve the matter of Philippa's wages, and give her a permanent home. Then Richard himself could give his whole attention to his work, and the dream of his life – his research in a place of his own. But Philippa had twisted her ankle, putting her out of action for a while, and she had developed a tendency to hysteria, which had only vanished when Richard had gone home. Impatiently he brushed aside what should have stared him in the face. For him, there was one thought only: he had found a girl after his own heart, in Sandra, tearing down the hill on that bicycle of hers, showing a zest for life that matched his own. They could have worked together, grown together with the years; they could have married, had fine sons…

He stopped himself dreaming abruptly, and remembered the glint of tears in Sandra's eyes as that elegant young man had bent over her, and casually kissed her.

Richard had never considered his was a jealous disposition, but the force of his feelings now shook him. He decided to do a round, to take his mind off things.

A new patient, put in a side ward for quiet, claimed his interest. An elderly woman, who had fallen heavily, sustaining a leg and head injury, though the cause of the fall was query cardiac failure following a shock, and she was listed as Miss Evadna Darley of Darley House.

At Nosterwell, everyone did a round. The cardiac specialist had been to see Miss Darley, with her own private doctor. Another heart man had taken his students in, and she had roundly said she didn't mind being prodded if it was going to help those young men pass their examinations, which got her a ripple of laughter because half the young 'men' were women with practical short haircuts and workmanlike heavy frames to their glasses. She laughed gently when her own doctor had pointed this out. Richard saw her at a time when laughter was far away. She had been thinking about Sandra, reflecting that she was in this same hospital, but seemed many miles away. This hospital rambled endlessly. Miss Darley didn't even know which floor her favourite niece was on.

She looked at Richard and decided he was a man she could ask. 'There is something on my mind,' she said firmly, 'and I am not likely to get over this if I cannot clear the burden from my shoulders.'

Richard sat down beside her, in that cosy way he had, and said he had lots of time to listen to her if she wanted to tell him about it.

'Then I'll tell you it all from the beginning,' Miss Darley said. He believed her. Sitting up in bed in her hand-embroidered nightdress, with the padded satin bedjacket that made her look much plumper than she was, Miss Darley was no more capable of telling a story straight through from the beginning, than the vicar's wife was. But Richard wasn't to know that. So when she said, 'There is an unfortunate girl in this hospital, who never looks fit to be seen, but who has had an unfortunate accident, and as she is under my care…' it really sounded logical and straight forward.

Richard thought at once that he was right. Sandra's aunt was an old retainer, even though she was now retired, and this rich old person was determined to help Sandra. So was he.

'Do you mean Sandra Stevens?' he asked at once.

'Ah, you know her,' Miss Darley said. 'What do you think of her?'

'I think she's a kind warm-hearted girl, though rather rash at times. But she's got a heart of gold.'

'A heart of gold?' Miss Darley repeated.

'A heart of gold. Do you know, before her aunt visited her–'

'Oh, her aunt visited her, did she?'

'Yes, finally, but the poor old dear was rather nervous and quite sure her niece would get them both into great trouble. But that girl, although her hands were bandaged preventing her writing, went to endless trouble to dictate a letter to her aunt that wouldn't give her a shock about her own condition.'

'Did she!' Miss Darley said thoughtfully.

'And has she told you all about herself, this girl?'

'No, not nearly as much as I would have liked. I met her one day when she came down the hill on her bicycle. My word, that girl enjoys life. (Well, she did enjoy life!) I don't know how much she'll be able to tear about when she's discharged from here. She wants to be a nurse, I understand, and someone should tell her she won't be anywhere near fit enough. Why, what's the matter, Miss Darley?'

'Leave my pulse alone, young man,' she said, smacking his hands off. 'I've had enough medicos around me today for one stretch of hours. You just sit still and talk to me. *How* will Sandra be, when she's discharged?'

'She'll have to rest for many months. I don't know how she'll be able to do that. She can't have much money, and her aunt is retired now, I understand.'

'I shall see to the money angle,' Miss Darley said. 'But don't let her know, please. And don't let my niece Audrey know.'

'That would be the pretty girl who came to visit Sandra, and put a lot of floral offerings and gifts all over the bed,' he suggested carefully.

'That would be my niece Audrey,' Miss Darley said. 'Tell me, what happened? How did Sandra like such a visit and such gifts?'

Richard flushed a little, and looked down at his hands. 'Well, it was just roses and things at first – no visitor – and, well, Sandra just threw them out. Put them on the tables for the whole ward, she said.'

Miss Darley chuckled. 'She would! And when my niece Audrey visited her? How did she react then?'

'I didn't see it all, actually,' he admitted. 'She was making a fuss about being put in a small ward, alone. Wanted to be left on the main ward. Then this fellow came in and showered stuff on the bed and kissed her… She seemed upset.'

'He's treated her very badly,' Miss Darley said. 'Oil and water don't mix,' she finished angrily, thinking as always of herself and her family as trade, and the St John Byrne family was the very reverse, and the mixture being entirely unsuitable in every way. Richard thought she meant that Martin's family were snobbish about marriage with servants and that his intentions hadn't been what Sandra had expected, and that that was why she had been upset. It made him angrier.

'If she cares for the chap, I don't see why–' he began.

'She was sick and silly over him,' Miss Darley said roundly. 'I can only hope that she has found out her mistake by now, and is being sensible. Now, that is what I want you to do, young man. What *is* your name, by the way? You have it on that brooch thing, but I can't quite see...'

Richard told her his name and got up. 'I'll keep an eye on Sandra for you,' he promised, 'but the thing is, I don't believe she's aware you are in this hospital. Is there any reason why she shouldn't know?'

'Good heavens, yes, of course I don't want her to know! Oh, and see to it that my niece Audrey is kept away from her. Poor Sandra is at a shocking disadvantage there. She'll only get the worst of it.'

She was well aware that Sandra would get the worst of it now that Audrey could flaunt Martin's defection in her face, but Richard, who had started off with a misconception of it all, thought she meant that the servant's niece could hardly have a stand-up fight with one of the family, who was doing her Lady Bountiful act in hospital. Personally he thought Sandra would probably give a very good account of herself, but this was a

117

cardiac patient of Sir Humphrey's, and he wasn't going to argue with her. He promised recklessly he'd do all she said, and went away feeling considerably happier. As he reached the door, Miss Darley called, 'Oh, and the money's all right. No, on second thoughts, don't tell her so!'

Again Richard misconstrued, and thought Miss Darley was under the impression that the small rooms at Nosterwell had to be paid for, as was the case in the smaller hospital in Brunchurch, but it hardly seemed worth bothering her with such details, as she seemed happier, suddenly, on mentioning the word 'money', and she was a cardiac case, so he nodded cheerfully, promised firmly to do just as she wished, and went out.

But Miss Darley had been thinking of the vast fortune that had at one time been promised to Sandra, and now had been shifted to Audrey.

She lay there with her eyes closed, thinking about it. Two hectic spots were in her cheeks, and she felt suddenly very ill. What had she done? Over the years she had come to the belief that if you had no social standing but a great deal of money, it balanced, because so many people with social standing nowadays had very little money. Like Martin's family. Sandra, without a good background and birth, must be given the lion's share of the money. That was what she had always thought. But she had been angry with Sandra, and bitterly disappointed, and had changed her Will in a fit of temper. On the strength of the change, Audrey, hearing about it from her irate aunt, had promptly managed to pull off her engagement with Martin. Now Miss Darley didn't feel she could retract, yet she passionately wished she had left things as they were.

What would happen if she died this night? A thrill of fear went through her and she at once rang her bell, to ask for pen and paper. But these were denied when the ward sister took one look at her.

Miss Darley said, 'Don't you understand? I must change my Will, or a terrible injustice will be done!'

The ward sister had heard this sort of thing many times during her nursing life and remained unimpressed. The thing was to save the patient, and never mind contacting solicitors, which would only excite the patient beyond help. She promised Miss Darley anything she wanted, and went away leaving her with a nurse in the room.

Nothing was to disturb this patient, she insisted, and the girl nodded. She had seen rich old ladies making a fuss before.

So Miss Darley lay and fretted and wondered what she could do, and thought of the wording of the new Will and the plans she had made for Audrey's Marriage Settlement, and that she had told the girl. Of course, she supposed, she could destroy the new Will, which would make the last one in Sandra's favour valid. She thought about it and remembered she had kept it, and never destroyed it. She had been in a temper that day and told the lawyers she had thrown it out, torn it up, finished with the whole thing. So they had taken her word for it and made the new one for her to sign. But, she thought, her heart banging painfully, if she did revert to the old Will, that would mean that Audrey wouldn't get Martin in marriage. Martin would come back to Sandra, and that nice young doctor (who clearly thought Sandra was the penniless niece of a one-time servant and obviously loved her for herself) would go away. Miss Darley could tell he loved Sandra, the way he spoke about her. It was more than she could have hoped for. He would hold Sandra down in the future.

But did Sandra love him? Much more likely that she would go back to Martin with open arms if she had half a chance. In tears, was she, when that wretched young man had leaned over and kissed her! Miss Darley was furious. He was such a cunning young man, she told herself, and only the rising and frightening ill feeling made her stop considering Sandra's future, and succumb to the enfolding arms of welcome sleep, with the matter of that vast fortune still un-resolved.

But it pleased Richard when he looked in on her later. She looked tranquil, and the ward sister was no longer worried, though she told Richard of the earlier panic, and she seemed half-amused. Richard thought Miss Darley was going to alter her Will, but he didn't realise it was to have again been in favour of Sandra.

Sandra… Ever since he had first seen her, she had been on his mind. Now he felt even more tender to her. She had had a rotten life, he considered. She should have been brought up at the vicarage, where his aunt and uncle would have cosseted and spoiled her. He thought of the future, and whether she would be any happier if she consented to be his wife. In his mind was the thought of a better job that had been offered to him but it carried no hopes of research and he had turned it down, but it was still free and with Sandra in mind he had applied for it again. He must have enough to support her in better circumstances than her life below-stairs, and in a small terraced house in Brunchurch, had held for her.

He half decided to look in on her and see if she was sleeping. It was quiet just then. Lights had just gone out. All the wards were in half light, with the pool of light over the desk of the nurse in charge. The side wards were in darkness. It was a half light and peaceful world, with the temperature slowly falling, and the clatter of daily life in a busy hospital giving place to the soft swish of rubber soles on polished floors, the starched rustle of uniforms and white coats, the muted sounds of work still going on in the sluice, and the occasional clang of trolley wheels as a patient was being admitted. His footsteps turned to Sandra's little side ward, but almost at once he was *bleeped* to go down to Casualty.

The main ward was full so one of the beds in Sandra's small ward was to be made up. She lay very still, eyes closed, watching two nurses in beautiful co-ordination make up a special bed for a newly admitted Casualty patient. As they worked, they talked. Sandra sometimes thought the nurses were of opinion that the patients in the beds were just inanimate lumps, with neither hearing, sight, or understanding. They talked as adults might talk over the heads of young children: sure of movement and lifetime but equally sure of the lack of understanding which would have needed care in the choice of words.

It was so now. They might well have been in a ward of empty beds, for all Sandra's presence worried them. 'I think he's gorgeous,' one said.

'I think it's a shame,' the small dark girl muttered angrily. 'His father just has to raise a finger and send for him and off he goes. Never mind his own career here.'

'Are you sure it's his father?' the tall thin one countered. 'Me, I wouldn't be surprised if a certain person flings hysterics just to upset his father so he sends for our Richard to shut her up. I mean, it must be awful, having someone like that Philippa make a scene all the time.'

'Why doesn't he sack her? Oh, I know it's hard for even a doctor to get a housekeeper these days, but she can't be that good if she keeps throwing a scene and taking off to bed.'

'She doesn't do it that often. She's clever. And she isn't just a stranger. Some sort of distant cousin, hard up. If his father is like our Richard, the last thing he'd think of would be to turn her off if she hadn't a bean.'

'So what will he do? She'll catch him one of these days.'

'No, I don't think so. Rumour has it that his father wants her. She's very pretty, they say.'

'Clever, too, if she manages to get our Richard to down tools and go tearing home to see what he can do for her. I mean to say!'

They finished the bed and gathered up the sheets they had taken off. The tall nurse was still far from satisfied. 'Funny about that rich old Miss Darley's niece, though.'

Sandra almost betrayed that she was awake, she was so surprised. They had stopped at the foot of her bed while one girl refixed the pin in the bar that held her fob watch. 'All that talk about her changing her Will in favour of the other niece. Well, I thought that might make a difference to him.'

'How come?'

'You must have heard! He'd run a mile if

he thought a person was rich. Pots of money and the way people spend it – it sends him up the wall. No, he wouldn't marry money. Quite the reverse, they say.'

'And is it true, what they say, about the other one getting cut out of the Will?'

'Much good may it do her, where our laddie's concerned,' the tall girl muttered, as they hurried out.

Philippa… Her name hung on the air. Sandra pictured someone capable enough to be the older doctor's housekeeper yet pretty enough to make Richard go hurrying home to see her when she was ill. She had more than a head start, too, being in the family, however distant the relationship. Was she related on the side of Richard's father or on the side of the vicar and his wife, Sandra wondered. She was growing hotter as she lay there. Scared, too, as she realised what Richard Norwood had come to mean to her since that day when her bicycle had careered away down the hill. He had filled the gap where Martin had once been. Sandra had thought that was all Richard had been – the stopgap, the man on the rebound. Now she knew how untrue that was. He was the big thing in her life. She had been stupid enough to fall in love with him.

Footsteps came down the corridor. She listened for the clank of the trolley wheels but it wasn't the patient coming in to that bed so recently made up. It was Richard. She now knew his footsteps. She tried not to look at the door, but she couldn't take her eyes off it. She had to watch his face as he looked at her. Would it be true that he would have no use for someone who had been an heiress (for how could he not have heard the truth about her by now?) or would he merely be friendly in a casual way, because of that other person claiming his thoughts to such an extent, in his father's home? Either way, Sandra felt she couldn't bear it.

He came in so casually, her heart sank. His cheerful smile meant nothing. She had seen it, on the ward, for many patients. Old and young women, pretty and plain, all qualified for Richard Norwood's cheerful smile. Only at that time Sandra had neither noticed or cared. Now she remembered.

He strolled over to her bed. 'Hello, there, so you're still awake! Want me to write you up something to make you sleep? Don't be afraid to say. It'll be plenty hectic soon, when the new patient comes.'

She shook her head, unable to speak.

'Okay,' he said, 'if you're sure. Good girl.

How are you feeling otherwise?' so she said, 'All right. No more pain than usual.'

He nodded. 'Guess who I've just been talking to. A friend of yours. Well, I suppose you'd call her that. She's very worried about you. Miss Darley of Darley House.' He pulled the stool out and sat on it by her side but he didn't touch her. 'Why didn't you tell me your aunt was there?'

He meant that her 'aunt' had been a servant there, but Sandra didn't know that. 'I thought you wouldn't like it,' she said in a muffled voice.

'Now why should you think that?' He shook his head at her. 'You're not ashamed of your aunt, are you?' he said softly, thinking of that funny old bundle of black clothing who had turned on the grocer's wife in the next bed, for being inquisitive.

Sandra could only think of Miss Darley at her most autocratic and belligerent. 'People don't always understand her,' she managed. 'She was always very kind to me. At least, usually she was.'

'Well, she's certainly devoted to you. And Miss Darley,' he said, remembering, 'seemed to think her niece Audrey might bother you, and she said she was to be kept away from you. So you see, although you think nobody cares about you, they do!'

Now Sandra realised that they were talking at cross purposes. He apparently didn't know that it was Miss Darley who was her aunt. Somehow she must keep him from knowing, although what good that would do, if it were true that he didn't care for rich people, she couldn't see. But she wanted to know things, and she wanted to keep him near her. However he seemed towards her, she couldn't bear the thought or his getting up and leaving her. 'Where was Miss Darley when you spoke to her?' she asked carefully.

'Oh, of course, you wouldn't know,' he said, clapping a hand to his head. Only then did he recall that Miss Darley had said Sandra wasn't to know she was in the hospital. 'I shall forget my head one day,' he said, getting up, as if he had just thought of something. 'Oh, by the way,' he said, not looking at Sandra, 'that chap who brought you roses and books and things: friend of yours?'

Sandra set her lips. 'No. No friend of mine. Not at all,' she said firmly, so he said, 'Oh, good, I thought you looked a mite upset. You are doing so nicely. Can't have you being bothered by visitors. Best get some sleep now,' and with a comforting pat on her shoulder, he went out of the ward.

Sandra wouldn't let herself call him back, yet there were so many things she wanted to know and hadn't asked. He hadn't told her where Miss Darley had been when she spoke to him. He hadn't told her how long Sandra herself would be in this hospital. And ... much more important than any of those things, he hadn't indicated that she meant anything at all to him, by word or look or touch. It was as if that day at the vicarage had never happened. She could only think that Audrey or Martin must have told him.

Or ... perhaps he had just been being friendly, and that it was true what those gossiping nurses had suggested.

This seemed to be born out when another house surgeon came round the following day, and when she asked the ward sister, in muted tones because of the silent, very ill patient who had been put into the third bed, where Dr Norwood was, the ward sister had said casually, 'Oh, didn't he tell you? He went home for a few days. His father is the local G.P. in his village. We live in fear that our Dr Norwood will one day decide to leave the hospital and go back to private practice.' That was what she said, but in Sandra's head, it sounded like, 'Our Dr Norwood will leave the hospital and marry Philippa, a relative of his in his father's house.'

FIVE

He hadn't found out any of the things he had wanted to. He paused in the corridor outside, wondering whether he should go back and ask Sandra outright: was she still in love with Byrne, why was Miss Darley so interested in her, why hadn't she told him of the connection with Darley House, why did she get into the newspaper and of what interest could she be to the press, and why was the young heiress so interested in her that she came to visit, when quite clearly such an act was not really her way of going on? To Richard there was some significance in all these things which he had somehow missed. He thought, too, looking back, that Miss Darley had deliberately given him the wrong impression, though he couldn't put a finger on it. And then he had to give up the problem because of another call. The sound of the *bleeping* was beginning to haunt him:

he couldn't even take time to think out a personal problem, these days.

He decided to go and visit the vicarage again. They had liked Sandra very much, and he felt that if he talked with them, quietly, they might put a finger on what was wrong, where Sandra was concerned.

He wanted to get it settled soon because there was the question of what would happen to Sandra when she was discharged from hospital. With any other patient, he would have told her, quietly but firmly, just what the position would be. But with Sandra, who loved life and who kept going at such an energetic pace, he flinched from telling her that it would be a long, long time before she got about again even normally. How could you tell a girl like Sandra not to think of riding a bike again, for instance, least of all freewheeling down that terrible hill? And where would she convalesce? Not in the tiny terrace house where her aunt lived, surely!

He didn't manage to get over to the vicarage after all. He received a call from his father. Philippa was in a bad state again. With a bit of careful wangling with a friend of his, the distracted Richard managed to exchange his next free time and get away to see his father that day. But he didn't manage to let Sandra know what had happened: she had more visitors – this time a professional man who looked like a solicitor, among them – and there was no way to let her know.

Richard thought of writing a note to her, but his own mocking thoughts jeered back at him – what makes you think she would want to know where you were, or care? So he left and the ward sister's careless explanation did more harm than Richard could ever have imagined.

He drove home with mixed feelings. He still yearned for that place of his own, where he could research as much as he wanted to, and he was in two minds about the job he had applied for. He had applied for it out of hand when he had first met Sandra and fallen in love with the hoyden on the bike coming down the hill. What would he do now, if it were offered to him? At the time, it had seemed simple. She had seemed to be a local girl, with no complicated life, and he had intended to ask her to marry him. It was as simple as that. She had hit him between the eyes and even his good aunt, who was vague enough in all conscience, had realised. He remembered Aunt Marion's kindly twinkling smile, and her comment: 'Whatever you decide to do, Richard, I hope it works out fine for you!' But it hadn't worked out fine at all. Who did Sandra like specially? That arrogant type who had been bending over her bed, and who was apparently already engaged to be married to Miss Darley's heiress? Or had it been the unfortunate chap killed in the accident, and in whose car it now seemed Sandra had been riding? He wished with all his heart that Sandra would be open with him!

And so he wasn't really ready for what lay ahead of him at home. Home was a Victorian villa, large, sprawling, with not much comfort, since Richard's mother had died. His father didn't seem to notice the house, and Philippa was unwilling to do more than what she was strictly engaged to do. Richard supposed the life of a working housekeeper to a doctor with a busy practice, was rather hectic, but at least she was living with a relative. Someone who cared about her welfare. His father was a kind, if absent-minded man.

He parked his car in the drive, and was surprised to find the door being opened before he had got there. His father, looking more grey and stooping than usual, stood there waiting for him.

'I'm glad you could come so soon, Richard,' he said, and came out into the little front garden and stood talking to him, about Philippa. 'I really am rather worried about her,' he said. 'I can't find what's wrong with her, and something's got to be done.'

'Well, if you can't find out what's wrong with her,' Richard observed, with a cheerful smile, because he was more worried about his father's appearance just then, than Philippa's hysterics, 'Then I don't know how you think I can!'

'Well, for one thing, you don't see her very often. I'm living in her pocket, as it were,' his father said.

Richard stood looking at the garden, so that he shouldn't betray his own anxiety about his father. 'What's the matter with her this time?'

'She doesn't eat, she tells me she can't sleep, and she's wandering about so listlessly, and, well, to be honest, she isn't doing any of the things she was engaged to do, and when I suggest getting someone else in, it starts her off again!'

'All right. You want me to have a look at her?'

'Oh, if only you would, my boy!' his father said in a relieved tone.

Richard nodded, and followed him into the house. 'Where is she?'

'In the room at the end, the one with the rose wallpaper,' his father said unwillingly.

Richard turned sharply. That was the best bedroom, the one that had been his mother's. But before he could say anything, his father said defensively, 'She finds it quieter, a more restful room. Well, if Philippa's happy, then I can get a bit of peace. That's all I ask!'

Richard went upstairs and knocked on the door. Philippa said in a spent voice, 'Come in! Who is it?' which seemed an odd way round to ask, especially as he had no doubt she guessed who it was, even if she hadn't heard his voice.

He opened the door, and stood staring. It was as if she had drawn into that room everything that was decent in the house, leaving the rest of the place, shabby, dull, with odd empty spaces. He let his gaze go round the room slowly, recognising things, pieces of furniture, pictures, oddments that had belonged to his mother.

Philippa said, a smile in her voice, 'Over here, Richard! Here I am!'

She was sitting in a pretty 'lady's chair', a Victorian piece now upholstered in rose pink plush, with a soft embroidered cushion behind her head. The late sunshine drifted through the window and touched her face. Not a pretty girl, but one who was oddly attractive. Oddly? The nose wasn't straight and the mouth was rather thin; the skin too white, the hair not any colour beyond a pale straw – long straight hair brushed to shine and tied back with a ribbon bow, giving a touch of blue which led to the illusion of very blue eyes. But the eyes weren't blue, they were coldly pale. Still, she was a girl who could make a man look at her twice, in spite of her absence of formal good looks and clever make-up. It was as if she were deliberately flaunting her lack of good looks, so that whatever attraction she was able to make, was made by her personality alone, and people looked again, to see just how she did it.

Richard said, 'Well, Philippa, they tell me you've been ill, but you don't look too bad to me!'

She smiled faintly. Nobody was going to persuade Philippa to pout or resort to any such feminine tricks. She looked coolly amused at him for believing what others said about her health. 'Come and examine me, doctor, before you start drawing conclusions.'

'But I understand that my father–'

'He hasn't examined me. He's such an old fuddy-duddy, he thinks it wouldn't be quite proper, and I personally will not have that other old fogey from the other side of the town, pawing me and humming and hawing.'

Richard frowned. His father was letting himself go but he wasn't going to have Philippa say such things to him. 'What seems to be the trouble?' he asked coolly.

'I'm unhappy, unwanted, overworked. Oh, I could list the whole lot of things, but I can see you wouldn't believe me. They call me the housekeeper, but that's a laugh. House-keeper!'

'My father thought it would spare you thinking of yourself as a poor relation, which you did when you first came,' he said un-compromisingly.

'Oh, I can see your father got at you before you came upstairs!'

He felt her pulse, laid a cool hand on her forehead, examined her tongue, and pulled down her eyelids. She chuckled.

'The old routine!'

'Well, Philippa, what do you want me to do? I could call in a nurse and give you a thorough going over.'

'Chaperone?' She leaned forward suddenly. 'You know what I want, Richard. You know, only too well!'

He stared at her, and thought irrationally and yearningly of Sandra, with her gay smile and her going into battle against the world, because she was unhappy. This girl was unhappy, but without reason. He said, 'I think I do, Philippa. You feel you're drifting. You want a life of your own, your own home, your husband and children.' All the things that Sandra should really have. He lowered his eyes so that he shouldn't betray to the world what he was thinking.

'Yes,' Philippa breathed. 'I knew you'd understand!' She leaned closer to him and put her hand over his. 'Then why don't you do something about it, Richard?'

He got up. 'I'm just thinking that I will, Philippa. Heaven knows, my father wants it badly enough. You must see that. He dotes on you.' He ignored the change in her expression, and said, 'If I could feel that you and he were making a go of it, and that you weren't going to be difficult about petty details like being my stepmother, I might feel better about marrying, myself. It isn't nice to have a worrying at the back of one's mind about one's father, especially if you'd only be sensible and make him happy.'

'I don't want him, I want you!' she sobbed, flinging herself down on the floor and burying her face in her arms, on the pink chair.

Richard said, 'My father needs a house-keeper. He's overworking. Are you going to do the job, Philippa, or shall I engage someone else? If I do, you'll have to look for employment elsewhere. You know the practice isn't a plushy one.'

'Don't I just!' she said, raising a drowned face to his. 'Why are you being so beastly to me, Richard? I've been *waiting* for you to come home. Waiting and longing! Oh Richard, don't you love me any more?' She suddenly flung out her arms, round his legs, as he stood beside her. 'Why can't it be like it was before? Why did you let someone else *change* you?'

He looked down at her in pure stupefaction, then he tried to unwind her arms from his legs. 'Don't be a clot, Philippa, it never has been *like that* as you call it! I'm seldom home, and I've been keen on … someone else … for ages. So cut it out!'

Then he saw the damage was done. His father stood in the open doorway and it was quite clear he was reading all the wrong things into what he could see, and telling himself he didn't have to think – it was all being enacted before his eyes.

'For heaven's sake…!' Richard began, but Philippa's noisy crying put an end to any attempt at explaining. Besides, the window was open and that sort of noise didn't sound good from a staid practitioner's house. Richard said sharply, 'Lie back, Philippa!' and as she raised her surprised face to look up at him, he gave her a sharp and telling slap across one cheek. 'Old-fashioned treatment for hysteria,' he said, 'and if you don't stop this nonsense, I've more old-fashioned remedies which we still practise at my hospital.'

His father closed the door on them and went downstairs. Richard said, in a bitter undertone, 'I don't know what all this is about, but I came home to ask my father's advice about something very important to me, and I am not going to get involved in your own private dramas. You either get up and be his housekeeper again, or get out. What's it to be?'

Her face crumpled again. 'Richard how can you be so cruel…' she began, then stopped in surprise as he walked purposefully towards his bag and got out his hypo syringe and two little bottles.

His father was in the surgery, staring out

of the window when he went downstairs.

He didn't turn as Richard went into the room and closed the door behind him.

'Dad!' Richard said sharply.

Then he did turn, but there was nothing of friendliness in his tired face. 'What happened? It's mercifully quiet,' he remarked.

'Quiet which you need, badly. How long have you been like this, Dad?'

'I asked you a question, Richard. What happened?'

'I sedated her. Long enough to give me time to talk to you about a problem of my own. I'm sorry, Dad, but Philippa's your worry, not mine. You'll have to sort it out for yourself, and don't send for me again, next time she raises another clincher. Deal with it. Show her who's boss. She might just look at you with new eyes. She won't if you keep trying to pass her off on to me.'

'She's in love with you.'

'I can't help that. I've got my own problems. There's a girl I want to marry, but I can't very well, while I'm worried about your health. I asked you before: how long have you been like this?'

His father shrugged. 'Since you last came home, I suppose, and that must be all of six months.'

'It's too long and you know it. Why the hell didn't you call in someone to have a look at you? Charring's a good chap and I could think of others.'

His father snorted. 'My dear Richard, you must know perfectly well there isn't a doctor breathing who willingly goes and asks another chap to examine him. We're all cowards. Much rather not know.'

'Then I shall personally send someone to you. You can't go on like this. Besides, I might not be in the country. I've applied for a job in Africa.'

It was a shock to his father, he could see. 'Dad, for heaven's sake, you've known all along what I wanted to do. I'm not getting anywhere at my hospital. Besides, there's Sandra.'

His father nodded, helplessly. 'Well, I suppose it couldn't turn out the way I hoped it would.'

'I hoped it would turn out right, too,' Richard said. 'Philippa looked young and strong and you seemed to like her so much. I thought you'd both marry and things would work out for you.'

'So did I, but she happened to meet you again, and she's thought of nothing else since.'

Richard looked angry. 'I don't even like her. I never did. You know that. People don't change much and she wasn't a likeable child.'

'Lots of children don't like each other, but do when they're grown up,' his father said hardily.

'Well, it isn't like that in this case, and I'm not coming home again while she's here.'

His father sat down tiredly. 'This Sandra – tell me about her.'

Richard thawed a little. 'She's a great girl,' he said, but he was seeing Sandra's thin pointed little face and her untidy thatch of hair, her zest for life when she was on that bicycle coming down the hill – a picture he could never erase from his mind – and the sight of her when he saw her in hospital after the accident with Benny, whose car and everything about him registered him as a member of the smart set that that heiress and her fiance belonged to. Richard never thought of it like that before and his father watched the anger crowd into his son's face again.

'And do you have to look so furious about this ... great girl?'

'Well, I'm not the only one who likes her so much,' he muttered, very unwillingly.

His father got up and came over to him. 'Oh. I'm sorry. Like that, is it? We're a fine couple, aren't we? Don't hitch our waggons to the right star.'

'It would have been all right,' Richard said, thinking, 'but something went wrong. I can't think what. There's something she doesn't want to tell me. Anyway, the poor kid's in no position to think much about what she should or shouldn't do. She's been in an accident and is in our hospital, in pretty bad shape, and I want to marry her.'

'Then you'd better sit down and tell me all about her and let's see if I can do anything to help you, even if you can't do much to help me,' his father said with a wry smile.

Richard didn't know where to begin, so he began with where he met Sandra, on the hill that day, and took her to the vicarage to get cleaned up. It turned out to be a far from good point at which to begin.

'What did you say her name was?' his father asked sharply.

'Sandra. Sandra Stevens.'

'But dash it all–!' he began, thinking. 'Look here, Marion has been on the telephone to me about that girl, since that day of meeting her. Very much taken up with her at first…'

'At first?' Richard asked quickly.

'Good heavens, yes. Enchanted with her. Then let's see – oh, yes, I know. She was on the telephone again with some nonsense about the girl being some rich old woman's heiress. Marion was very upset. Didn't know what it was all about or whether you even knew, on account of your strong views on inherited wealth, and all that.'

Richard stared, then burst out laughing. 'Oh, no, poor old Aunt Marion, she's got it all wrong. No, my poor Sandra is the niece of one of the staff at Darley House. The heiress is old Miss Darley's niece Audrey, who comes to visit her. Sandra doesn't like her patronising ways. Hardly surprising. Pretty girl, but quite insufferable, I should say.'

His father still look bothered. 'Yes, well, see here, something's not right with this story. Marion and her husband are pretty well known in the district – not just their own parishioners but everyone. There was a chap and his wife, the ones who were telling them. It seems there were two girls, one pretty, one a complete little tearaway. Marion says the pretty one wasn't the heiress, for some reason. Everyone talked about them, wondered why old Miss Darley didn't do something about the other girl, curb her ways, so to speak. Hardly an advertisement for such a wealthy old party. But there, Darley's Dog Biscuits. And that's not all. There was a fortune come from ironmongery, not quite sure which. Well, the old girl was pretty well loaded, one way and another, and this little tearaway was to get the lot, and yes, it's coming back to me. Got her engaged to one of the St John Byrnes – that's right! Of course, they are just about down and out, financially. Pretty good thing for the boy to be engaged to the heiress. I don't suppose they cared what she looked like or what she got up to, so long as they got their hands on her money.'

He got up and poked about in his desk. 'I remember now. Marion actually wrote to me about it, and that was why, I suppose. Thought she saw interest your way, in this girl, and got upset when she discovered the young lady was already engaged to be married. And then it comes out … yes, here's the letter. It seems there was an awful row because the other girl, the pretty one, fancied the Byrne chap, and they were carrying on behind the other one's back. Yes, I never did hear how all that finished. And you say that's the girl you're keen on? No, Marion must be mixed up. Hey, where are you off to, Richard?'

146

Richard quietly got his coat and his bag and went out to his car. He hadn't much recollection of starting up the engine. He did remember seeing his father standing on the front doorstep shouting at him, but he was starting up the engine, backing out on to the road, and didn't want to stop. All he wanted just then was to get away somewhere quiet, where he could think this out. He had a sinking feeling that there was the ring of truth to his father's narrative, that had been sadly lacking in other stories he had heard about Sandra, particularly the one from her own lips.

SIX

The sum total of his cogitations was that he should have believed Miss Darley when she had said that Sandra was 'sick and silly over that chap', because Sandra, for whatever reason, had certainly looked very upset when the fellow had leaned over her bed and kissed her. Richard's rage consumed him. He had got the whole thing wrong, hadn't he? Sandra had kept from him that she was the heiress and that Miss Darley was her aunt. But then, what on earth had that pantomime by the bedside been about, when the old servant had visited her on the open ward that day?

Now his thoughts were swayed again. Aunt Marion must have got the story wrong, or someone must have told her the wrong thing. Because if she *had* got the story right, then it meant that Sandra, his Sandra, his fun-loving girl who had swept down the hill into his life that day, had been deceitful, deliberately leading him to think that she was what she was not. But then, his thoughts swayed, if she *were* the heiress, surely she must be a consummate actress to carry off that ragamuffin air? She was being an ordinary girl and enjoying it. Nobody could possibly act like that!

He gave it up, but decided not to go back to the hospital for a day or two. He had got the time off and he was in no mood to go back and face Sandra until she was nearer to getting up, and until his own thoughts had clarified a little. Until, too, Miss Darley was more fit to talk to him, and do some clarifying herself, he finished grimly. Of his father and Philippa, he thought nothing. His whole thoughts were taken up with Sandra and the queer set of circumstances surrounding her, and the two days he took off, fled.

He tried to picture Sandra, what she was doing, whether they had got her up for a little, which was what was to happen. She was young and healthy and her bones were knitting together nicely. The principle of the hospital was to get the accident patients moving as soon as possible.

The accident... Ah, yes, there was the curious business of her being in the car of the chap who'd died, a man subsequently named as Benjamin Wakeman, who was a friend of Miss Darley's heiress, a young man known to be on the look-out for a rich wife, so Richard had been reliably informed by colleagues before he had left the hospital to see his father. A young man who Sandra had been heard to mutter about in her delirium, and to name as 'Benny'. She knew him as well as that!

Now Richard's thoughts were taking him to the other viewpoint, against Sandra, and he could only picture her receiving those rich friends at her bedside, and possibly going back to the man she had once been 'sick and silly' over. Sandra beginning to get about again, performing her first two or three steps to this man's delight...

Sandra was not performing for anyone. She had been taken, at Miss Darley's request, to see her. Sandra with splinted limbs and a bandage still round her head, supported in a chair being pushed by a young nurse, was not a pretty sight. The ward sister had warned Miss Darley what to expect, but it was till a shock to a recently recovered cardiac patient.

'Not too long, and no upsetting Miss Darley,' the sister warned.

They were left together, and Sandra sat wooden-faced, afraid to speak in case she broke down. This was the old aunt she had been so fond of, and who had been secretly brought into hospital. Why hadn't she been told?

Miss Darley said, 'You naughty girl! What have I planned so much for you for, to have you spoil it all?'

The injustice of it struck Sandra, and she spoke before she remembered that quite possibly Audrey had already given her version of everything, and it would be twisted to suit herself. 'I didn't want anything planned. I just wanted to be me, liked for myself!' Sandra burst out.

'Liked by whom?' Miss Darley said wrathfully. 'Poor Benny Wakeman? And look where it got him! Don't you know that people like us are not liked for themselves but for what they are worth?'

'Then why did you make me your heiress? Why didn't you let me be?'

A nurse looked in, at the raised voices, but for the moment they were just staring stonily at each other, so she went out again, leaving the door ajar.

Miss Darley said, 'You were the one nearest and dearest to me.'

'So you never believed a word I said, but preferred to listen to Audrey!'

'At least Audrey did talk to me, miss, and not avoid me, as you did!'

'What's the good of being talked to, if what you're getting is only half the truth?' Sandra retorted. Then she closed her eyes and shook her head wearily. 'I'm sorry. I shouldn't shout at you. I've only just been told how … ill you've been. I didn't even know you were in hospital. That wretched Dr Norwood wouldn't tell me where you were when you had spoken to him.'

'What did he tell you I'd said?'

'A lot of rigmarole that made him think I was the daughter of an old servant and that you were interested in me and would keep an eye on me.'

Miss Darley chuckled. It was so unexpected that Sandra's eyes shot open in surprise. 'He's such a dear young man,' Miss Darley said. 'And quite clearly he doesn't really listen to elderly ladies telling him their troubles, but he appears to be listening and it's very flattering.'

She stopped smiling and said fiercely to Sandra, 'We haven't long to talk, so be good enough to tell me, very briefly, just what had been happening, from the day of your birthday when you came in to lunch in those dreadful clothes.'

It was going back too far, but Sandra suddenly longed to tell someone all about it. But not about the trip to the vicarage. That was secret, rather special. So she thought a moment, then said slowly, 'I'd been on the maid's bike. It was fun. But I fell off, and got taken into someone's house to clean up my scratches and the dirty patches. I was in a bit of a mess, and I got given a lift back.' She carefully edited the story, and told it with expression. 'Then I put on the things I'd bought myself. I wanted to feel I could be an ordinary person and wear just what I liked on my birthday, only you didn't like the things.'

Miss Darley, with terrific restraint, just listened, trying to understand this dear niece who had so disappointed her. She said nothing, so Sandra continued, 'Then Audrey and I said a few things to each other – well, it was a bit of a row, actually, and I was fed-up and went out...'

'What did you both quarrel about? You'd better tell me because I have other informants, and it is essential for me to get at the truth.'

Sandra slowly went ashen-white, as she said, 'Oh, yes, other informants. Don't I know that! Well, if you must have the stark truth, Audrey let me know she and Martin were in love, but he meant to marry me to get the money and we were to make a cosy three-some in the future, me saying nothing, them doing as they liked together. That was the crux of the matter. I was fed-up and went out, and someone gave me a lift.'

'Benny!' Miss Darley assumed erroneously, and Sandra decided it would do no good at all to upset her aunt by correcting her, telling her about the near-disastrous 'pick-up' with the commercial traveller, from which poor Benny rescued her. 'Wakeman's lazy lout of a son! No, I mustn't say that. The poor lad's dead, and it won't help. You didn't feel you could like him, did you?'

'I didn't think about it,' Sandra said

frankly. 'All I wanted, all I ever wanted, all I ever will want, is to be liked for myself, and I'll never do that with your money hanging round my neck, so I have to tell you I'm glad you made Audrey your heiress. I'm glad she's going to marry Martin. I'm glad I'm … *free*.'

The sister came in, to terminate the interview, but as they were so quiet, and neither of them looked upset, she softened and acceded when Miss Darley begged for another few minutes, to say something *very important.*

'Very well, just another few minutes,' the sister smiled and went out.

'Nobody is free, child,' Miss Darley made the effort to say. 'And you have been brought up in a certain way which hasn't fitted you for marrying some young man who thinks he loves you for yourself, and can earn enough to keep you.'

'I can learn a trade or something!'

'Listen, child. We have so little time. I *heard* the row between you and Audrey, and I was so grieved, I collapsed. When I was ill, I wanted you to come and you didn't. Nobody told me you were injured and in hospital. I thought you didn't care about me. In a fit of temper I made over a lot of my money to Audrey, and young Byrne snapped her up. They're a fine pair. Do you mind?'

'Losing Martin? No. I discovered I hated him for presuming I'd be willing to be his wife even without love. He thinks so much of himself! I loathe him!'

Miss Darley nodded. 'So I did right. Audrey has the dog biscuit fortune. There is still the Tugwell money, and a large number of small warehouses I've bought up since. Enough to see you'll never want, for the way of life you've been brought up to–'

'Don't you understand? *Won't* you understand? I don't want it. I want none of your money! Work it out for yourself! Audrey said I'd never know which I was being married for – me or the money. Well, it's the only truth she's ever spoken. So let me find out if someone wants me!'

'Child, you'll be disillusioned and hurt again!'

'No! Leave me be! If someone wants me, he'll have to work hard to get me. It'll be a real conquest, because I shall make it hard, so hard. I just have to know, to be sure, that he loves only me. You keep out of it, with your money – give it to Audrey, all of it! I want none of it.'

'We need not let anyone know there is a lot

of money coming to you when I die,' Miss Darley pleaded, but Sandra's face set hard and her eyes had no liking in them at all.

'You want to rob me of the only chance I ever had to find out who cares for me! I'll tell you something. I was plain and un-attractive before, and totally without charm. Well, now I've got some more disadvantages that will make the test of a man more difficult. They haven't told you, have they? I don't know if my face will remain scarred, but I'm certain of one thing: I shall have a limp, for always. So if someone proposes to me, ever, I'll know he really wants me.'

It was a shock, but Miss Darley hung on, and saw her solicitors when she had again recovered. Tenacious about the infallibility of her own planning, she also had a great fondness for Sandra for the girl's own dis-position, but there was, too, a fondness for Sandra's late mother. The two were very much alike. Miss Darley was determined to cushion her niece against the follies of her own muddled thinking. Sandra would never be able to earn anything, especially since it was apparently true that she would indeed always walk with a limp. So she arranged with her legal advisers that it should be put about that she had quarrelled with this niece again, and there was no money for her in the future: at the same time she arranged that the bulk of her money should be for Sandra, on her marriage.

'It's a bad arrangement,' the elder solicitor said, in a distressed voice. 'If it ever leaks out, your niece will be prey to all the adventurers – worse than if you had just named her as your co-heiress.' But Miss Darley merely got excitable and her solicitors were sent away. So nothing was arranged, and she was kept from her legal advisers for a long time. As things stood, there was nothing at all for Sandra, not even Darley House.

The bulk of the fortune was still settled on Audrey and her fiancé, and the Byrne family were waiting to swallow it up in putting in order Byrne Place, the surrounding estates, and paying off the masses of debts. Audrey and Martin had a quiet wedding one wet day when Sandra was edging herself along between two bars in the rehabilitation centre, and wondering where her brave words were going to get her, concerning her earning a living.

Miss Darley, in a rare patch of strength, had agreed to Audrey arranging her own marriage. There was no sense, she told herself, in waiting for her own death. Audrey might not manage to catch the young man of her choice if someone better suited to him came along, for the Byrne family were now in a bad way financially. Audrey's marriage had been hanging on too long, to please their creditors. Her Marriage Settlement was sufficient to please Martin's family, and he knew that they would at least have half the remaining fortune on Miss Darley's death. And she was very ill indeed.

It was supposed to be a quiet wedding, because of Miss Darley's health. Sandra looked at all the magazines and newspapers, in one of her rest periods, and read about Audrey's trousseau. The young nurses were full of it. They had all seen the beautiful Audrey and her handsome beau. Now they read out chunks of descriptive pieces about the clothes designed for her by an Italian genius. 'I thought the best clothes came from Paris!' one said, but another was reading about Audrey's hair styles, and someone else professed more interest in Audrey's car, a wedding gift from her in-laws. It filled the conversation of patients and nursing staff alike, for two or three days, but not longer. Other things splashed on to the hospital scene to take away their interest, so Sandra could smart in peace. Even Mrs Franey had been discharged and gone home without bothering Sandra again. But nobody said what had happened to Richard Norwood and Sandra wouldn't ask.

On the day that Miss Darley made a further effort to persuade her solicitors to make that controversial new Will, Sandra managed to persuade the ward sister to set in motion an application for her to try to work in the Appointments Department. 'I can learn to be a clerk, surely! And I'm good at figures and in hospital nobody will think anything of my limp, will they?'

That was the day that two girls in the Appointments office went sick so Sandra had her chance. 'And please don't let Miss Darley know – it's an absolutely special reason why I don't want her to know!'

The ward sister thought sentimentally that it was to be a surprise, the rich young woman who always looked anything but rich, proving to her aunt that she was capable of doing a job like anyone else, so she conspired with Sandra, and Miss Darley knew nothing of it. She had worries of her own. Richard had come back, and called to see her before he looked in on Sandra.

'I wondered what had become of you, dear

boy,' Miss Darley said playfully. 'You didn't say you had a holiday!'

'My cousin was ill and I went home,' he said slowly. 'And then my father collapsed. He's been secretly ill for some time. But I've got someone I know to look him over. I think he'll be all right.'

'I'm glad,' she said. 'People ... they are so strange. They never do what one expects. Now my dear niece Sandra...'

Richard sat down slowly by her side. 'Sandra Stevens is your niece?'

'Why, yes, didn't you know? But you must have done! You talked to me about her before you went away!'

'I talked to you about Sandra Stevens. I thought she was related to one of your domestic staff, the old woman who came and pretended to be her aunt,' he said, the friendliness dying from his eyes, just as Sandra's had done that last time she had seen Miss Darley. Miss Darley took fright, and was convinced she was handling these young people the wrong way.

'She's very proud. Not like her cousin Audrey. Audrey doesn't mind who knows she's rich. Not so Sandra. Sandra likes to be considered an ordinary person.'

Richard said slowly, 'I see. Then it was all

a tissue of lies.'

'What was?' Miss Darley asked him sharply.

'The day she came to the vicarage and charmed my aunt and uncle. The vicar prides himself on knowing people. Instinct he says. He was way out over Sandra!' and he laughed mirthlessly. 'I was, too. I thought it was such a happy day and that she was such an honest, truthful girl.'

'Well, she is! When was this? She never told me–'

'Well, there you are, do you see! She forgets to tell people the essential truth. Did she tell you she gave the address of a small house in a poor street at the back of the town, and which now turns out to be your servant's address, and not hers at all? I imagine that Darley House was her home address.'

'Yes, but–'

'And did she tell you about her accident?'

'Yes, and if you think she had any thoughts of that young waster marrying her for her money, she was all against that happening, whoever the man was! Oh, I know he's dead, but I never thought much of him and I know his father was always keeping an eye on the private fortune that was to be settled on Sandra. And now I'm going to settle the rest of my money on her too. She tells me she'll always have a limp and–'

Richard got up. 'Miss Darley, I think if I stay any longer, you'll get excited, and that will not be good for you. I am sure your niece Sandra is all that you say and believe her to be. I expect it's my own stupidity that got the wrong story, so please don't worry about anything. Where is she now, by the way?'

'In her room, I imagine. Isn't she?'

'I'll find out,' he said, going to the door.

She was frightened. He hadn't said, 'I'll go and find her,' but 'I'll find out,' and he had made it sound so formal, so perfunctory. And she had just realised that he was more than interested in Sandra – at least, he had been, on that other occasion – and Sandra had winced when his name had been mentioned. Was this the man that Sandra really wanted?

'Dr Norwood!' she called, and was shocked to hear how feeble her voice sounded. 'I must ask you–'

He came back, courteous as ever, and stood by her, waiting.

'Are you back for good, now, or is it true what they say, that you'll go back into private practice?'

He smiled politely. 'I haven't made up my mind.'

'You see, they said you wanted to do research. Someone did, I can't remember. And I would like to donate – well with so much money, surely you could use some–'

She was being clumsy. Something she had said offended him. His face closed and he said, 'Excuse me, I have to go now, and you are really talking too much. Try to get some sleep,' and he left her.

She could have cried. She was so used to managing people, so used to getting what she wanted by mentioning cash. Everyone had his price. Where had she heard that before? In a long difficult and not always happy life she had found it to be true. But it didn't seem to be true in the case of this young man, nor in the case of Sandra. She fretted all day for her solicitors to come, but they weren't allowed, and she began to fear that she would never get that new Will made, and it would be too late.

Later in the day she asked firmly about Sandra. 'I want to arrange for her convalescence, and for something to be done to eradicate the limp she is so sure she will be left with,' she said angrily.

Only the threat of getting over-excited, got her the service she wanted, and finally it was arranged that Sandra should be sent to a place called Maplegate where there had been some property Miss Darley had been interested in buying for some time. It hadn't been a great desire of hers to push through the deal, but now, since Sandra needed country air and had this all-consuming passion to work for her living, she thought it might be a good plan. Since the ward sister had promised Sandra that her new little job should be kept secret, and since the hospital wanted Sandra to be kept reasonably close to Out-Patients for constant treatment and to see that she didn't go back to her old careless ways, nothing much came of the idea, and Miss Darley grew angry and frustrated, and her condition worsened.

That day Richard went down to the Appointments Section without knowing Sandra was there. Nobody was queueing. The clinics were finished for the day. Sandra was leaning exhaustedly against a filing cabinet, searching for the place for a fat bulging file to be put away. She turned as he spoke, and her face lit up. But he didn't notice it. He was only aware of the scar that ran from her eye down the side of her face, and the way she had lost that healthy tan, and her cheeks were hollowed, her hair lank, and her shoulders sagging. Where was his energetic, enthusiastic, fighting Sandra?

Because all these thoughts were fighting in his mind, and the constant doubt as to whether there was any truth in Miss Darley's (and others') assertion that Sandra was indeed a very wealthy young woman, he didn't smile. His face was set, his eyes brooding. Sandra's heart sank.

'Can I ... do something for you, Dr Norwood?' she forced herself to say.

'No. No, not a thing. I came ... actually to look up something. I can find it myself.' But that meant going in there, to that filing cabinet she was at, and he couldn't. He wanted to take her into his arms but he also still smarted over all she hadn't told him. 'Never mind,' he said, walking away.

Sandra couldn't believe it. Whatever else he had been like to her in the past, he had always been most courteous. To walk away like that! She was tired and discouraged. That day a new bogey had raised its ugly head: it wasn't enough to expect pain until she got used to being about on that injured leg of hers, nor was it enough to expect a perpetual limp. Now she had to fight the other enemy – fatigue. The more she was on that leg, though they insisted the exercise was what she needed, the more fatigue would creep in, and with it the throbbing that was so much like tooth-ache.

She dragged herself to a chair and sat down. Slow tears coursed down her cheeks. She had longed for Richard's return with an ache that was in itself even worse than the pain in her leg. And now he had returned and was going to be cool, not even polite to her!

Sister Macklin found her stifling sobs that wracked her thin body. 'Now, now, Sandra, all the time you were on my ward, you never did give way to tears,' she said rallyingly. 'Although perhaps it might have been better if you had!' she finished thoughtfully. 'Mop up, now. I want you to come with me. Someone wants you to have tea with them.'

Sandra's head shot up. Not Richard? Of course not, she flayed herself savagely. Her great-aunt? Oh, not, *not* Audrey and Martin!

She had been saying those things aloud. Sister Macklin smiled. 'No, you silly girl. Two people who say they are old friends of yours. I seem to recall they visited you once or twice before. A Mr and Mrs Vennall. He's a vicar, of a village near your own, he tells me.'

She looked stupefied. Why should Richard's aunt and uncle come to take her to tea? 'Just those two? Nobody else?' she insisted, and when Sister Macklin smilingly agreed that it was indeed just the two of them, she got very slowly, draggingly to her feet.

'Okay, I don't mind,' she said. 'I hope someone's told them about my scar and my limp.'

Sister Macklin helped her rinse her hot face in ice-cold water and tidy her hair. 'Oh yes, we've told them what you look like, that you're quite fierce about your few disabilities, proud of them I sometimes think! You funny girl! They must be good friends of yours. They didn't know you were still in this hospital. Come along!'

Sandra said bitterly, 'I can't think why. Dr Norwood could have told them. They're his relatives!'

'That isn't to say he's been seeing them lately nor that he tells them about every patient in the hospital,' Sister said with mock severity. 'If they hadn't come, I was going to ask you to take tea with me.'

'Why?' Sandra flung up her head. 'Oh, that isn't polite, but it struck me that you

167

thought I might be … might be…'

'As lonely as I would be, if I had your job and got left to hold the fort,' Sister said briskly, as she guided Sandra to the front hall.

Marion and her husband rose as they saw her coming. They didn't seem to know what to say at first, so Sandra said feebly, in the current jargon that the vicar so deplored, and that Marion helplessly allowed she would never be able to catch: 'Hi!'

Marion's answer was to go over to Sandra and kiss her cheek, and say, 'We were so sorry to hear you are still here, my dear. We thought you'd gone home– We did so much enjoy your visit to us that day. We want you to try out a new restaurant we've discovered.'

They matched their pace to hers, as she slowly walked with her stick to their car, Sister Macklin on the other side of her. She looked neither pleased nor sorry to be going out; rather, Sister Macklin thought, as though she were determined to endure everything, even an invitation to tea. And all the time Sandra kept thinking to herself, 'He looked really put out to see I was here. He'll go back and get his file now, now I'm not polluting the place. He probably told his aunt and uncle to invite me, to get me away!'

It was stupid, childish. She knew that wouldn't have happened. She knew it was quite likely that Richard didn't even know his aunt and uncle had come to the hospital. He had probably had a bad day. It probably just a case of the first time she had seen him put out, and it was probably wouldn't be the last. But it didn't matter now, she told herself, and tried to tear her mind away from him to listen to Marion's conversation.

The vicar drove carefully out of the hospital grounds, and to the outskirts of the town, where the quiet residential streets began, and then he drove into the forecourt of one of those family hotels that looks almost as discreet as a dwellinghouse itself. He parked with precision, and neither he nor his wife made the mistake of trying to help Sandra out of the car until she dropped her stick. Then the vicar picked it up and handed it to her and remarked cheerfully: 'Had a young parishioner who copped it with his motor cycle and if anyone tried to help him he swore most colourfully. Not saying you'll swear at me, Sandra, my dear, but I'm not taking any chances,' which made her laugh, and after that it was all easier.

In the past she had liked ice cream and creamy pastries, but since the accident everything had gone: all her old tastes, even her appetite. They saw this and said nothing. Marion ate her share with determination and a total disregard of what it would do to her already comfortable figure. The vicar talked easily, until his wife decided it was time to talk about the main topic – the one which they had decided to put to Sandra today.

'It's a sort of holiday for us really,' she smiled at Sandra. 'Getting away from the parish to dally over tea in another place. But there is business in it, and I'm afraid it's really my fault, what happened, and I've got to put it right or I shan't sleep.'

At once Sandra was wary. Marion saw this. 'Now, my dear, let me say what I have to, or I shan't get back to it again and I'll have no peace. We liked you so much that day Richard brought you home, and we didn't know who you were, and we have so much wanted Richard to–'

Sandra could almost hear the kick the vicar aimed at his wife's ankle to warn her she was on the wrong tack. Marion hastily tried again.

'Well, the thing is, my clot of a brother – Richard's father, that is – is wonderful at handling his own patients. (You know he's a local G.P.?) But he really hasn't a clue as to how to handle his family. I told him something in confidence...'

It wasn't going well. The vicar leaned forward. 'Sandra, didn't you want Richard to know who you were?'

Sandra warmed to him. 'Of course not,' she said simply. 'I fell over backwards not to let him know.'

'That's what I thought,' the vicar agreed. 'How long did you expect that to last? And what did you think Richard would say when he found out ... as he surely would?'

'That's neither here nor there,' Marion broke in wrathfully. 'The thing is, we were told by some interfering busybody that you were the rich niece of old Miss Darley, and it seemed such a shame ... well, knowing how Richard felt about inherited wealth ... so I got in touch with my brother, to find out if Richard knew. The thing is, Richard's father never listens, never takes the trouble to read anyone's letters closely...'

'He hasn't time,' the vicar smiled, 'to sort out what you're really trying to say, my dear,' and his wife flushed. 'And if we're not careful, Sandra will get up and take off, before you've finished trying to explain just what you mean.'

'No fear of that,' Sandra said gruffly. 'My leg hurts too much. Oh, not to worry. It always does play me up at the end of the day.'

The vicar said, 'Would you like to come and sit out on the terrace in the cool? There's a little breeze.'

'No!' Marion put in quickly. 'I believe Sandra's like Richard – when there's action, you never get them back to the subject and I want to finish explaining. Besides, I want to have some more tea, even if Sandra doesn't.'

'Sandra will think we're very impolite, to invite her to a tea she doesn't want, to tell her distressing things she doesn't want to hear,' the vicar said quietly.

'It doesn't matter,' Sandra said dully. 'I expect if he hadn't found out at home, Richard would have found out some other way. Anyway, it makes no difference. There never was anything in it. I've heard he's going to marry that cousin of his, Philippa something.'

'Oh, no!' Marion said, much distressed. 'She's for his father. My poor brother is silly over her. Did you hear this from Richard himself?'

'No. We're not on such terms that he can discuss with me who he's going to marry,'

172

Sandra said coolly. She turned to the vicar. 'Tell me about the animals. I did so much enjoy that day at the vicarage.'

'Yes, I think you did, my dear,' he said, slowly. 'I suppose we couldn't persuade you to come and stay there for a week-end or something? Richard won't be coming, no fear of that.'

Sandra thought about it and was tempted. 'If I went anywhere, it would be where I was sure I wouldn't know anyone, or be known. I don't think you could promise me that, could you?'

'Why don't you want anyone to know you're an heiress?' Marion couldn't resist asking.

'I'm not an heiress,' Sandra said fiercely. 'My cousin Audrey is. She got the lot and I'm glad. I want to be just me, and behave like everyone else, choose my own clothes, my own friends, and not have people saying I look a fright, in spite of all the money. I know what I look like. I don't care.' She broke off in exasperation as Marion still stared, her good-humoured face puckered, not understanding. Sandra turned to the vicar. '*You* understand, don't you? That day I came to you, was fun. Know what I mean? In my oldest clothes, my hair standing on end, and riding the maid's bike. Nobody would let me have a bike. If I went anywhere, it had to be in the Rolls, chauffeur driven.' She swallowed. 'Ordinary rich people don't have to behave like that, but we're trade, d'you see, so we have to put on the style ... so my great-aunt says.'

'And you don't like having to put on the style,' the vicar said gently, smiling his nice smile at her.

'No, and I loathe being reported in the press. It's as if they know I can't make it successfully and they have to be there to report each time I behave badly. But not any more. I'm just Sandra Stevens, with a scar and a limp, and nobody will want to see me in the papers.'

The vicar thought differently. He went outside to say a few words to the cub reporter who had spotted Sandra, and naturally wanted to follow up her accident with the question for his readers: why did Sandra Stevens get cut out of her aunt's Will, and is she really cut out after all?

'Why don't you leave her alone, Jimmy?' the vicar asked. 'When I helped you get this job, I didn't expect much, remembering what you were like in the choir, but at least I never thought you'd persecute someone who's been through so much!'

'I'm not, Vicar!' the young man protested.

'Then why are you so keen to report her taking tea with us? She's in pain, and not interfering with anyone! Why can't you leave her alone?'

'She's good for even a line or two, any day,' Jimmy said, shrugging. 'I'm sorry she's going through it at the moment, but come a few weeks and she'll be racketing around, and someone else will get the story, which I don't mind telling you, Vicar, goes down well! Well, she does racket around!'

'But what's so special about her? Why can't you chase other rich young women, the pretty ones?'

He grinned wider. 'This one's a lad. She looks like nothing on earth, and, well, Darley Dog Biscuits. But what she gets up to! It's as much fun as when someone wins the pools and goes berserk. See what I mean?'

'Yes, I see,' the vicar murmured, leaving him.

Marion was waiting to tell him something. 'Sandra really has been disinherited,' she said, in doubtful tones.

'Come to us for a week or two, my dear. At least you won't be pestered by anyone, and you look to me as if that Sister was right –

not enough sunshine and relaxation, too much devotion to your filing cabinets. All right, I agree you now have to work, but the hospital wants you to convalesce, and if you're not so well, I can run you in to the Out-Patients department in no time at all. What do you say?'

Sandra looked at him. She was so tempted, but wouldn't there be heartbreak that way, with Richard's presence everywhere in that vicarage, all mingled with the memory of that one wonderful day? On the other hand, if Richard were going to be about the hospital, as he was today, and she risked seeing him at any time with that set look on his face … no, she couldn't bear it.

'Well, if you're sure Richard won't come,' she said.

The vicar said wryly, 'I think I can almost promise that. We've been wanting him to come for ages now, without much hope. No, he'll be shuttling between the hospital and his home, I'm afraid.'

They arranged everything with the ward sister when they took Sandra back, and it was settled that she should spend two weeks with them. She went upstairs to say goodbye to Miss Darley, a sort of duty visit.

Miss Darley was hurt. 'You wouldn't

accept the holiday I arranged for you! It was to be so nice, and a sort of job for you to do, as well, since you have this stick-necked desire to have none of my money!'

'Let's not quarrel, dear aunt,' Sandra said, wishing that whenever she saw Miss Darley these days, her aunt didn't feel so antagonistic.

'How can I help it? I have nothing but my money to give you. Don't you know that when a person means a lot to you, you feel you have to give and keep giving?'

'*Why* do I mean so much to you?' Sandra forced herself to ask, so that by the very argumentative nature of the question, she could keep her mind away from the needle-sharp question her aunt had just put to her. Of course she wanted to give, to the one she loved! She wanted to give to Richard all the time, but she didn't know what to give. He seemed so self-sufficient. Even in old clothes, at the vicarage, he had seemed to have everything. That was it: an aura of contentment surrounded him. Did this explain his dislike of inherited wealth, because he believed a person couldn't be content with something thrust on them, without having earned a penny of it?

Miss Darley said, 'I've never told anyone

this before. Your mother was so dear to me, and you are so like her. You grow more like her every day. She wasn't quite as ragged-headed as you are. She had nice hair which she brushed but she never cared for fine clothes or the social scene. And I loved her, and she was taken away from me. But she left you for me. And you've rejected me, constantly rejected me.'

'Only because you tried to make me over into what you want, aunt!'

'Don't you understand anything, Sandra? I wanted you to have all my money because Audrey had everything else: beauty, charm, a way with the men; gifts, like her music and all the other things she was so good at. You had nothing so I had to make it up to you somehow. And you've never let me.'

'If you'd have given me the one thing I wanted, I'd have adored you. I would! I really would! I wanted freedom. No, don't say nobody has freedom. They do. Lots of people do. And when they're allowed to go free, they come back home, because they're not afraid of being trapped into staying. I'd have come back to you if you'd let me go.'

'Go where? To make friends with servants and their families?'

'There you go again! Not specially servants,

though I don't see what's wrong with them. Melchett's an old dear, and she loves me. She did everything she could to help me. I could have been happy with her.'

'With Melchett?' Miss Darley was scathing. 'You are my own flesh and blood. I was going to take you on a cruise … it would have been nice for me, too. I was going to buy you so many things. You'd have liked a car of your own, wouldn't you? I don't see why you've always stood out against my gifts.'

'No, you don't understand,' Sandra breathed, seeing her aunt for the first time. You could spend the whole day explaining what you meant, but like the vicar's wife, Miss Darley only saw her own point of view. But at least Richard's Aunt Marion didn't get truculent about it. 'Anyway, I came to say goodbye to you, because they think I should go to the vicarage and have a lazy couple of weeks.'

'And then what?' Miss Darley asked, her mind working very fast. Why was Sandra consenting to go and stay with the aunt and uncle of that Dr Norwood, when she wouldn't snap up the offer to go to Maplegate, which was so near his father's home?

'Then I'll come back to the hospital and

my job,' Sandra said, with decision. 'A job I shall like because I know how to do it and I shall do it properly and be paid just what I'm worth.'

'Well, you can tell people you're not an heiress if you like,' Miss Darley said, lying back.

Sandra's head jerked up. 'You mean you've decided not to– Oh, it won't do any good, anyway. People who know the connection will never believe that you've grown so much away from me that you can really mean to cut me out of your Will.' She sounded so dispirited.

'If you are thinking of that young fool, Dr Norwood, he is past considering as a sensible person. I keep hearing people say how he saves every penny for his research, and I offered him a decent sum for building a place of his own and–'

'Oh, no, Aunt!'

'There you go! You are against me, too!'

'Oh, don't you see? To approach him, a total stranger, and offer to finance his own pet thing, without even discussing it with him–'

'And what was there to discuss, pray? Either he needs money or he doesn't and according to everyone I meet, the nurses swoon at the sight and sound of him and know all about his being too hard up to do his own pet thing. So why can't I mention it, and try to help him?'

Sandra got up. Her aunt watched her, with pain at her heart, while this dear niece struggled with the stick, managed not to drop it, and got herself somehow, to the door. This dear ragamuffin, who had been so quick on her feet, so vital and alive and tearing about, enjoying the sunshine like a leaf being skittered along on the wind. And now she could hardly move...

'Sandra! Are you not going to kiss me goodbye?' she asked, unthinkingly.

Sandra turned carefully, measured the distance between her and the bed, and couldn't face the journey back. It was the end of the day, she was too tired, too emotionally worn out, too grieved about Richard Norwood, too everything, especially too surprised that her aunt hadn't thought that it was dragging her back, all those extra effort-filled footsteps and movements of painful limbs. 'No. Consider I've kissed you goodbye already,' Sandra said.

SEVEN

The Rectory looked a little smaller, Sandra thought, and Trudy looked less huge and good-natured, but then it was a washing day and it had been showering and the washing had had to be rescued three times, so, Sandra thought, she couldn't expect to find things all serene. And it was a bitter-sweet return, because she kept remembering Richard.

Because of Sandra's stick, they used the wash place on the ground floor. If anything, it was better, cleaner, than the family bathroom upstairs. She supposed it was either easier for Trudy to get at, being so near the kitchen quarters, or perhaps it was for Trudy's use mainly, so she had a greater interest in looking after it.

Marion came in with Sandra. 'I'm sticking my neck out. I'm sure you don't need help, but Trudy's in a bit of a mood, so I thought it might speed things up if I were near at hand in case...' and she smiled comically, well aware of how her over-helpfulness affected people.

The scent of good cooking mingled with the scents wafting in from the garden, the way the plants and grass smelt after summer showers. Marion said, without stopping to think, 'Why did you pretend so hard, the first day?'

Sandra was goaded to say, 'Because I was batty about Richard and didn't think he'd like me if he knew about Darley's Dog Biscuits.'

Marion nodded. 'But how come you didn't see him afterwards, to explain? Oh, my dear, I like you both so much and he isn't happy, you know.'

'That's hardly my fault. I didn't ask to get in an accident almost at once, and anyway, he could have asked me!'

'Richard doesn't ask. He's not like me. He really is discreet and very thoughtful of other people's feelings. Besides,' she broke off with a sigh, 'I don't know exactly what happened, having had three different versions, but he could be feeling you hadn't been open with him.'

Sandra set her lips mulishly. She didn't like all this questioning, but she saw how Marion felt. Richard was a very dear nephew, she could see. 'He could have spoken to me about it. He would have found out that I didn't like inherited wealth either. But he never did.'

'That's because you wouldn't tell him how you came to be in that young man's car, especially as his father said openly in the press that he was hoping his son might cut the other young man out.'

'He never did! Not Benny's father! I don't believe it! No, he wasn't so nice – that wasn't what I meant. I meant that he was wrapped up in his business and despised poor Benny and he wouldn't have known what Benny was doing, or what he was capable of. He always said Benny was a lazy good-for-nothing.' And she remembered that Miss Darley had practically said the same thing. 'Oh, well, he probably was hoping to cut the Byrne family out!'

Marion had the good sense to stop there, however. She brought the kittens to be inspected. They had grown from the tiny puff-ball stage and were now lean and mischievous, running up the curtains and clowning, conscious of Sandra's laughter. Marion looked as if she were personally responsible for making Sandra laugh. The vicar, however, looked thoughtful. Sandra's laughter had the quality of near tears to it.

He wondered what his wife had been saying.

They had arranged for Sandra to occupy a folding bed in one of the odd reception rooms on the ground floor. It opened on to the garden where the strawberries grew, and soon the mother dog brought her puppies, and they played in and out of the room, keeping Sandra happy.

There was a spell of fine weather. Sandra helped the vicar sort his papers, and helped Trudy cut up vegetables and fruit, and as the lazy hot days stretched ahead, she took to going to the meetings with Marion, so long as she could sit down all through. She liked the Jumble Sales, and the lively life of the church. She sat in on a Brownie meeting, and made friends with the young organist – Tony Johnson – a new young man in the district. He was to take Sandra home in his ramshackle car after one of these meetings, as Marion had promised to deliver some of the things they had taken, and might not be back within the hour. Sandra couldn't get through a whole day without resting on her back. And the organist's car wouldn't go.

Sandra sat on a stone into which the last of the old metal chains formed the edge of the burial ground, and watched his efforts.

He was bent double under the bonnet, happily pulling caps off and reporting on the state underneath them, and that he would soon get the car to go, and take Sandra back, when a long shadow fell across them and a voice that made her heart turn right over, said coolly: 'No problem. I'll drive Sandra back to my uncle's,' and Richard unsmilingly gave his arm to Sandra who was already scrambling to her feet in confusion.

He glanced quickly and disinterestedly at her, and walked her slowly to the road, away from the protesting organist. But he was so upset inside that he stopped supporting Sandra as soon as they reached level ground. It was agony to touch her and stay cool and calm. 'How are you, Sandra?'

'Fine,' she muttered, red-faced.

'They didn't remember to tell me where you were, or I could have come before, and done chauffeur duty.'

'It isn't necessary! The vicar drives us over,' she said in a hurry.

He closed the car door on her and hurried round to the driver's seat, as if he had hardly time to drive her anywhere. 'I shan't be long at my uncle's. It was just to say goodbye. I'm going home.'

'For how long?' she asked, in spite of the

lump in her throat that made speaking difficult.

'It's hard to say. My father's ill. I've contacted a chap who thinks he can help him,
but he hasn't returned from the States yet.
My father shouldn't have left it so long.'

'Doctors do, I'm told,' Sandra offered.

He nodded, and for no reason pulled up in
the space in front of a field gateway and sat
staring across into the haze of a hot afternoon. The countryside smelt sweet and good.
Sandra had the odd feeling that she would
like that day to last for ever.

Richard said, 'Do you like staying with my
aunt and uncle?'

Suddenly his formality offended her. 'You
don't have to be polite to me. You didn't
have to give me this lift. You were very over-
bearing with poor Tony, and he means so
well. He can't help it that his car's old and
has to be coaxed.'

'I wonder you didn't arrange to have the
Rolls and the chauffeur to drive you around
every day,' he said.

Angrily she faced him. 'Do you honestly
think I like that? Why do you think I was
messing about on an old bike that day?'

'Rich girl playing at being poor, because
she knew she didn't have to continue with

the farce when it palled?'

She swallowed. 'How come you were so good at pretending to be the nicest man I ever met, that day at your aunt and uncle's? I wouldn't have thought anyone could act that good, and then be such a stinker afterwards!'

'I'm sorry you feel that way about me. I can assure you I was not pretending then and neither am I now. I just deplore that you weren't more honest with me at the time.'

'Oh, and what would you have said and done, if I'd said to you, "I'm not really having to ride this bike. It's just fun for the day. The chauffeur will come and get me now I've crashed it."'

'You could have told me who you were.'

'You wouldn't have believed me. You wouldn't have even if I'd let you drive me back to Darley House. You'd have thought I was one of the maids, the same as … the same as the man did who gave me a lift and then tried to be funny,' she flared, though she hadn't meant to say that. 'Yes, you didn't know that, did you? I'd just discovered something that made everything collapse.'

'How could you?' he retorted. 'You'd got everything laid on. Even the engagement with the handsome man your aunt was so pleased with!'

'You're not up to date with your facts, are you? Or won't you believe what you hear? I'd just heard from my cousin that he didn't want me for myself but just for the money. It was my cousin he was in love with. Yes, that surprises you, doesn't it? What did you think? That I threw him over, for fun? Just what did you think about that marriage of theirs?'

'I had your aunt's version,' he said tautly, his thoughts racing. Which man was this? The one who had been killed in the car, or another one? He never read newspapers, and never listened to gossip, certainly not about Sandra, who had been lodged in his mind as the niece of that old party sitting by her bedside.

'Well, he married my cousin and I thought she'd got all the money, but now my aunt says she didn't make it all over to Audrey. How do you like this story? I was engaged to be married, that day I was at your aunt and uncle's. I thought you were all a lovely family and that I was sitting on top of the world because the man I loved, loved me. Martin Frenstoke St John Byrne loved me, I thought. Only he didn't. He loved my cousin Audrey. And now I know I didn't really love him, and I don't know anything at all. Nothing's worth while. People are hateful. And I can't get about, like I used to. I could tear about, forget anything that worried or hurt me...'

She turned sharply away and struggled to keep her composure, while Richard cursed his inability to find time to read newspapers and keep up with local events. Everyone must have known that she was to marry young Byrne. Now he began to see the significance of that spiteful piece in the gossip column which the patients were reading and talking about. He turned to her, and then he realised another thing: she had been engaged to be married, that day, and he, poor fool, had fallen in love with her and wondered why she hadn't been more open with him.

Flaying her because of the deep hurt he had just sustained, he said, 'So now we know why you pretended, why you weren't open with me. You were going back to your rich aunt at Darley House and your fiancé only you didn't want to spoil your day out slumming!'

It was all much much worse than Sandra had ever thought it could be. She could have said that she hadn't been *officially* engaged to be married, and that she hadn't known that her cousin was then going around with Martin. She could have said she wasn't very happy at Darley House and that was why she escaped sometimes. She could have said that that had been the happiest day of her life – her birthday, and the day she had met Richard and his aunt and uncle, and that she hadn't seen the significance of that meeting until she had got back to Darley House and realised she couldn't get Richard out of her thoughts. She could have said any or all of those things but her throat was too tight, and his manner hurt her unspeakably.

Finally she managed to say, 'Please drive me to your uncle's. Now!'

From the depths of his own misery, Richard said, 'I'll do that, with pleasure! And in passing, I don't think I'll ever trust a young woman again! Not ever!'

Not even Philippa? her thoughts screamed, but she couldn't put them into words. How dared he talk to her like that, when all the time he was due to marry that Philippa, who all the nurses were talking about, and for whom he had thrown up everything at the hospital, the minute she was ill?

'Perhaps nobody will trust you, either!' she snapped. 'You've got a nerve, talking to me like this, when all the nurses are taking bets on just when you'll marry your cousin Philippa!'

He had started the car up, and the road was no longer quiet and clear behind him, so he had to keep going. She could tell how angry he was, because his face was white, and a little nerve twitched near his mouth. They travelled in uneasy silence back to the vicarage.

The sun was burning down, drawing out of field and garden a hundred drenching heady scents. The birds were more noisy than Sandra remembered them; the puppies, half grown but still gangling and awkward enough to fall over their own feet, tumbled out of the house towards the car, then spotting a kitten, changed direction, and yelping, charged in the other direction and vanished into the bushes. The vicar stood at the window of his study, half in shadow, willing Sandra and Richard to lose that anger in their young faces, and to be in accord with the summer and the birdsong.

Richard turned to her. 'I'm not going to marry Philippa. I'm not going to marry anyone.'

'Then you'd better do some correcting, or people like me may get the impression that you prevaricate as much as you accuse me of doing.'

'Wouldn't you say you weren't honest, that day you came to us, knowing you were engaged to be married? I thought you were–' and he broke off.

'I hadn't met anyone else except Martin. It seemed all I wanted, until I – heaven help me, until I met you, only I think I must have been very much mistaken. You've made me as unhappy as he has.'

Hot angry words rose to his lips at what he considered the injustice of that remark. He said shortly, 'I'll take you in, before we quarrel again!' and before she could argue with him he was out of the car, round to her door and lifting, swinging her in his arms and marching to the house with her.

She was so light weight, it shocked him. Little and somehow beaten, her hair standing up on end in tufts that were somehow comical and yet heart-tearing. Like the rest of her. She fought, yet underneath it, she was as truthful as he wanted to believe her, and very sweet.

He put her down. 'I've got things to do. Now don't say a word – or we'll be fighting again. Just let things be!'

She pulled herself together. 'You've got a nerve, the things you've said this day,

193

Richard Norwood! You've deceived me ever since I first met you. I've just remembered – you even kidded me along you were a tatty old First Aider when all the time you were high up the surgical ladder at the hospital! And I couldn't count the number of other things you've deceived me over–'

'At least I've never let anyone think I was free when all the time I was engaged to be married! I've never let anyone think I was anyone else but plain Richard Norwood–'

'Plain Richard Norwood! That's a good one! Why, you–' she said hotly, but suddenly, without being able to help himself, he caught her to him and kissed her, hard. Having started, he couldn't stop kissing her. She was so astonished, and limp with emotion that she put up no fight at all, and he kept on kissing her, until the vicar, wondering what had happened at the sudden cessation in their sharp-tongued battle, came out into the hall, and they sprang apart.

'Just going, uncle!' Richard said, on a gasping note, and put Sandra away from him so sharply that she lost her balance. He was running to the car, and didn't look round. She tried to regain her balance, but couldn't, and slid down the wall to a sitting position on the floor, half laughing, half crying.

The vicar muttered, 'Young idiot!' and helped Sandra up. He wasn't a small man but he couldn't swing her up into his arms as Richard had done. Between them, the setting of her on her two feet was such a sorry business that he finished up in helpless laughter, Sandra leaning against him.

'Well, at least you're laughing, my dear!' the vicar said, as Richard's car roared down the drive and into the road. 'I thought you were going to cry!'

'I thought so, too,' she admitted. 'Oh, Mr Vennall, he kissed me!'

'Well, why not? You're a nice little thing. If I were his age, I'd kiss you, too, and I wouldn't push you over in my haste to get away afterwards!'

'You can kiss me now, if you like,' she said recklessly, so he did, fondly on her forehead. 'Is it congratulations, my dear?'

'I don't know,' she admitted, and somehow found her cheeks were wet. 'I'm afraid you came out too soon. He didn't get round to saying anything. He was just wild with me.'

'Oh, I see,' the vicar said, in an odd voice. 'Come in and sit down in my study and we'll call on the excellent Trudy for coffee or tea or something. Bless my soul, I've forgotten what part of the day it is.'

They went and sat down, and Sandra had time to think. Richard had been indulging in a reflex action, hadn't he? He hadn't said he loved her or that that kiss was anything but the culmination of a wave of anger and frustration. She sat looking at her hands, thinking it over.

'Well, my dear?' the vicar murmured, at length.

'I was thinking. I told my aunt why I didn't want any of her beastly money. I told her that if any man wanted me, I'd know it was for myself, but he won't find it easy. He'd have to conquer me.' She looked at the vicar. 'I didn't think I'd ever be a doormat. I don't think Richard will have to do much conquering.'

'You really have refused your aunt's money?' he asked slowly.

'Oh, yes! And she understood, too. She believed me. She was so furious. I suppose I shouldn't have made her cross – she has a heart condition – but I had to convince her that I really meant it. I had to make her see that I have my life to live and she has no right to spoil it. I wasn't wrong, was I?' she finished anxiously.

'I'm sure you wouldn't intend to make

your good aunt angry,' he said slowly, 'but forgive me, I find it hard to understand your attitude regarding wealth. I'm afraid I haven't got Richard's advanced ideas on the subject.'

'Advanced?'

'Yes. I believe it is modern to take the attitude that inherited wealth is not to be enjoyed or – er – endured. I believe that if I inherited a fortune, I would be humble and thank heaven for it, and set about doing some sensible things with it, both for myself as well as for others.'

'It isn't like that,' she said slowly, wondering how she could disabuse him. 'In a way Richard is right, I suppose. I mean, if I chose to have my great-aunt's fortune, I wouldn't be allowed to live my life as I wanted to. I would be expected to entertain a lot of people I didn't like, and wear a lot of clothes I hadn't chosen but which were considered the thing, and I'd have to pattern my life to fit. D'you see?' But of course, he didn't. In his simple, honest fashion, he was thinking of the repairs to the Rectory that a fortune would enable him to make. It never occurred to him that he wouldn't have to work and wouldn't be expected to stay in the living, but might have to get out and make way for another clergyman.

Sandra could see that. Everyone seemed to think this way. She shook her head. 'I think I'd better pour, hadn't I?' she said, and thought about Richard and wondered what he was doing. He would go back to the hospital, and bury himself in work and get over his mood and then wish he hadn't let it happen, she decided, swallowing hard on the lump in her throat.

Richard had certainly gone back to the hospital, but not to work. He wanted to see Sandra's aunt. He learned that she was much better and to be allowed up the next day. If she made progress, she would be sent home soon. The atmosphere of the hospital, and the lack of communication with her solicitors, was not doing her much good, the sister said.

Richard went up to her room, and met with a welcoming smile from Miss Darley. 'Ah, there you are, young man! I was just thinking about you!' she greeted him.

'Good afternoon, Miss Darley,' he said quietly, and pulled out the stool from under her bed. 'I was hoping to have a quiet talk with you.'

'About my niece Sandra?' she guessed, and if he hadn't been so engrossed in what he had to say and how he was going to frame the words, he would have noticed that she was fairly excited, and he might have learned that she had already had some unsettling visitors: Audrey and Martin. They were back from honeymoon and wanting to know just how much Audrey would be worth in the future, so that, as Martin delicately put it, they could base their style of living. Miss Darley had said roundly that she was quite sure what they meant was how much would they be left in her Will when she died, and that she wasn't dead yet. It had all been rather upsetting, though they hadn't raised their voices.

'About your niece Sandra,' Richard said. 'She's not happy.'

'Bless me, that child won't be happy, either, because she can't tear about and look as if she needs a good wash. Sooner or later she must learn to mend her ways and look like my heiress should look!'

He stiffened. 'What did you say?' he said on a low note.

She thought about it. 'You think she is no longer my heiress, perhaps.'

'Isn't she?'

'Let's begin again,' Miss Darley said playfully. 'Just what did she tell you? Repeat it word for word.'

'She said she had told you she didn't want your money and that it was an agreed thing between you.'

'An agreed thing! Ah, now I understand you!' Miss Darley said comfortably. 'She was indulging in her old argument – my dirty money – but finally we parted great friends, and agreed to *say* that she wasn't going to inherit. The silly girl, what could she hope to do by way of earning her living? Why, she won't earn as much in wages as would cover her cosmetics bill, let alone her dressmaker. As for the Rolls and the chauffeur…'

Richard got up, his eyes like flints. 'You both agreed to *say* to any interested party that she was not going to inherit, but she is really going to inherit. Am I right?'

She thought of his need for money for his research project, his place to work in, and estimated what his salary at the hospital must be, and she chuckled. Really, these young men were all alike. Full of pride and big words, but when it came down to brass tacks, they needed money the same as anyone else. Money talked. Money was something you could see and feel, something that gave security, confidence.

'I knew you'd see reason,' she said,

whacking his hand with her reading glasses case. 'Now, have you and Sandra agreed to make a match of it?'

'I think not, Miss Darley,' he said, putting the stool precisely under the bed, and straightening up so that she saw for the first time that his eyes were flinty, cold as ice, and his face set, as if in stone. 'I hope you will continue to make good progress.'

He was going. He wasn't going to marry Sandra. Sandra would find out what she had said and would be furious. Her excitement soared, and she felt that her throat was so large that she was choking. 'Dr Norwood!' she managed, but this time he didn't stop, nor look round. With his head filled with bitter thoughts about the way both Sandra and her aunt twisted things to make them suit the occasion and the time, he went straight out without looking back.

Miss Darley lay looking at the door. Her heart was pumping madly and pain filled her. She couldn't breathe, she couldn't call out, yet she must try. She must tell him three simple words: 'She didn't know!' because of course, she mustn't let him think that Sandra knew of her plan to leave her all that money. That was the essence of the whole thing: let Sandra think she was having her way, not inheriting, yet all the time the money would be there for her, when she would need it. Need it for operations on that poor little scarred face, and on that distressing limping leg.

She tried to call out, clinging to her consciousness, but she could hear his footsteps going further and further away. Then they stopped. Voices could be heard. She didn't know it, but the ward sister had stopped Richard Norwood with a query about Miss Darley. 'She has been doing so well and we have actually let her contact her home to discharge her tomorrow, but I wasn't too happy about the look of her after that other niece and the new husband came in. Mr Wills isn't in the hospital, so would you–'

They walked back together. Miss Darley, struggling to keep conscious with the hope of telling Richard those three words, heard the footsteps stop and saw her door open, and then she spoke. At least she tried to, but a strange hoarse croak was the only sound torn from her lips. She saw their faces change, saw them come rushing towards her, then the ward sister turned and ran the other way. She would be going to get the heart machine, Miss Darley knew, as she let the darkness slide over her. The heart machine, and she had the conviction that she would never be able to say those three words to Dr Norwood.

EIGHT

Richard was the one who told Sandra about it. It was the following day, and somehow the happy mood hadn't lasted. She had played with the puppies and the kittens, and helped Marion cook the big mocha covered sponge cake that the vicar loved, and they had together turned out more things from the drawers upstairs for the next Jumble Sale. Sandra had always loved the thought of going through drawers of forgotten and unwanted clothes. Nothing like it had ever happened at Darley House, where people's things were thrown out at the end of the season and collected for Miss Darley's pet charities. No fun in that; the maids attended to it, supervised by the terrible Mrs Lake. Sandra was still thinking about Miss Lake and the influence she had had in her aunt's life, when Richard arrived.

Even the weather had gone back on them

that day. Not exactly wet, but lowering grey skies, a chill in the air, and just enough moisture to make it necessary to wear rain-wear or stay indoors. Her heart did its usual absurd gymnastics at the sight of his car, but it settled with a sharp drop when she saw his face. It was that set look which she dreaded.

Marion and the vicar insisted on being with them while he told her about her aunt, too. Had that been Richard's idea, she wondered, and thought perhaps it might be, for the vicar, at least, was the soul of tact.

'Are you telling me my aunt is dead?' Sandra asked, after Richard had been carefully skirting round the subject. She didn't understand how difficult he found it to tell her gently, when the old anger had arisen at the sight of her. How could she look so calm, so normal, when all the time she had been cheating him again? Pretending she wasn't going to touch Miss Darley's money, when her aunt had openly admitted that they'd arranged between them to just pretend that situation was the latest arrangement, but that in reality she would inherit as it had always been intended.

'No, but she's very ill indeed. She had a close call,' he added.

Sandra was desperate. How could she talk

to him, when his aunt and uncle were in the room. She turned to them. 'Would you – I mean, could I speak to Richard alone for a moment, please?'

Richard didn't wait for them to agree. 'I'm afraid there isn't time. I must take you back to the hospital. I promised Sister Macklin I would, but then I have to go right away to see my father. As you know, he's far from well, and he talked to me on the telephone last night.'

His voice was losing its chill, and as if realising that, he closed his lips tightly, and said, 'Will you get ready, Sandra, please? And you come too, Aunt Marion, and I'll see if I can find someone to give you both a lift back. I don't suppose they'll want Sandra to stay.'

Gone went her hopes of talking to him in the car, too, but the vicar said quickly. 'No problem, dear boy. You cut off home if you're worried about your father, and I'll run Sandra and Marion in to the hospital and wait for them. I've got a fairly free day today. I'm glad Marion's going to be with Sandra,' he said, as he watched her drag herself out of the room and close the door behind her, his wife with her. It would take a little while for her to gather a few things…

'What happened, exactly? The last I heard about it, from Sandra, was that her aunt was improving so much that it was expected she would be allowed to go home soon.'

Richard turned to the window and stood drumming his finger tips on the sill. 'I think I upset her. It brought on an attack. She gets too worked up. She likes things the way she wants them, and gets furious if someone…'

'I can't believe that, Richard! I can't believe you'd cause an attack!'

'Oh, well, there it is. You see, I wanted to see Miss Darley about … Sandra and me. Oh, yes, yesterday was another day. We had a row in the car and sorted things out between us and I was going to tell Miss Darley so.'

The vicar looked so happy. 'My dear boy, so you're going to marry Sandra? You didn't tell her this, or that you were intending to see her aunt!'

'I am not going to marry Sandra,' Richard said flatly. 'Yesterday, perhaps … and it's as well I didn't tell her.'

'But why, why? If I may ask! She's such a dear girl, and yesterday you felt … you intended… What can have happened?'

'I still can't trust her, that's what happened. Oh, it's no use looking like that, Uncle. She's like that. My dear Sandra fools everyone.'

'I don't believe it. You must be mistaken, Richard!'

'Well, I'm not. Miss Darley nearly died, to prove it.'

The vicar looked absolutely aghast. Richard continued, 'I just went to tell her about Sandra and myself, and she at once took the conversation over and in no time at all I was hearing the one thing that smashed everything. It's no use your looking as if I've gone mad! The main point at issue was that inheritance. It always has been. I will not marry someone with a fortune of that size. How could I? I shall never be worth much and I'm not going to be known as the husband of the Darley Dog Biscuits heiress. Besides, I should be sucked into that world. I want Sandra to be dependent on me, and in my world.'

'Well, I understood that she now has nothing, which was why she is at such pains, literally, to keep that job at the hospital!' the vicar said.

'Yes, isn't that a laugh?' Richard snapped. 'Another of her wonderful acts! Her aunt said roundly that they had agreed to say she wasn't inheriting because Sandra has this theory that she won't know who wants her for herself or her money. (I understand the chap she really wanted, admitted it was her money that attracted him and that he was silly over the pretty cousin.) Yes, well, I know that must have been hard for Sandra to take, but there again, she never told me about it. She never told me she was engaged. She never told me she was Miss Darley's heiress. Dash it, she never told me anything!' He drew a deep breath, unconscious of how his voice was carrying, so that Sandra, having arrived at the door and was about to open it, heard it all. 'But that's not all of it. It's this situation now, pretending to be so hard up when all the time she's going to be so rich it makes my head spin to think of it. Not just the Tugwell Kitchen Appliances, but a few warehouses (her aunt said carelessly) that she'd bought up and made to succeed. Loaded, Sandra will be! And she's fooling me that she's penniless and needing me!'

Marion held Sandra's hand so that she shouldn't open the door, but Sandra broke free and threw the door open. 'You say I don't tell you anything,' she said on a low passionate voice. 'Well, you don't tell me anything, either, and you're quite right about not trusting people. I can't trust you! You just find out things and believe them whether they're right or wrong, and then you go off and simmer and sulk about them. All right, I don't know whether my aunt really meant it when I told her to cut me out of her Will and she agreed – it doesn't matter any more. Whether I'm rich or penniless, you keep out of my life, Richard Norwood. I don't want you!'

Miss Darley always said she had the constitution of an ox, and she had never ceased to be surprised that her heart should play up in such a way. This last attack had really frightened her. She promised herself she would never get angry and worked up again.

'Send me home,' she begged the hospital people. 'Send me home, with a nurse, and the appliances to deal with the next attack. It may not happen in my own home. I feel it's being boxed in a hospital room, away from the telephone and my lawyers, my own things, my friends – let me go home and I'll be better!'

It was worth trying, the doctors allowed. Anything would be worth trying, and the hospital was so short of beds, that they let her go, provided she had her own way and that Sandra went with the nurse and her aunt.

Her aunt had expected opposition. There was none. Then Miss Darley hopefully thought that the terrifying sight of the heart machine working, had probably made Sandra feel she must agree with her aunt's wishes down to the last detail, and that made Miss Darley very happy. She had no idea that the thought of going back to the kindly aunt and uncle of Richard, was the last thing that Sandra wanted to do. To forget Richard, was the thing she wanted most. It struck her that she might as well agree with her aunt, and accept the money, accept any adventurer who came along without caring which he wanted, herself or the inheritance. What, she asked herself desolately, did it matter? What did it matter if some young man ran through her money, and left her to find delights with some other girl, a girl blessed with a pretty face, and a talent for enjoyment. Sandra felt she would never enjoy anything again, as she stared hopelessly in the mirror at the scar.

It might not have been so bad if she could have got about again as she had used to. Walks in the wind, riding someone's bike, running with dogs, swimming, ice skating ... what did a person do, who liked to do those things, and no longer could?

In the weeks that followed, Miss Darley

kept calm, and reasonably well. Everyone thought she would now be all right. In time she was allowed to see the lawyers, and enjoyed herself very much going through all her securities and having fantastic ideas about what to do with them, and with Sandra's future. Sandra was now the centre of the life and every time Sandra appeared to look even faintly protesting, Miss Lake was always there to frown warningly, and remind the girl that her aunt's life hung on the slender thread of Sandra's good behaviour. It was like being in a prison, the girl felt.

Miss Darley, as she grew stronger, began to question Sandra, as she had in the old days. 'Do you ever hear from that young doctor, Richard Norwood, my love?' she asked confidently, as they sat together in the warm sunshine in the herb garden one morning.

Sandra wondered drearily how, while protesting that Sandra was the one person in the world who meant anything to her, her aunt could still hurt her so much, and trample over the few things she held dear. She said, 'No, aunt.'

'What a strange thing! I believed he quite liked you. I think I shall send for him.'

Sandra drew a deep breath to protest, then

remembered she mustn't upset Miss Darley. She shrugged, and said, 'As you wish.'

'You're not still interested? Well, that's no good, then, is it? I had hoped you still wanted him! Well, my dear, I have always told you that you can have anything you like if you have enough money, and you could, you know. Now don't get angry with me because I mustn't be upset, but I am quite sure that if that young man were shown a suitable place in which to do his research (that's if he really wants it!) he would succumb.'

With time, Sandra told herself, she would be able to put on an outer skin, really look as if she were unmoved. She would be able to prevent the hot tide of anger from running redly up her pale cheeks. She would not have to bite her lips so unmercifully to stop the furious words from streaming out when Miss Darley ripped everything wide open for inspection and rejection. Richard, succumbing to big money? It was the most hateful thought she had ever had put to her, Sandra told herself drearily.

'I did think that Darley House might be nice for him to turn into a big research station, after I'm gone.'

Sandra said, 'As you wish, aunt. I am not really interested. You're keeping very well so it really is very much in the future.'

To please Miss Darley, Sandra had started taking music lessons. She didn't much like playing the piano. She loved good music, and would much rather have sat listening to it than painfully trying, not very successfully, to play it. But to please Miss Darley was the order of the day. Miss Darley now said, 'How did you upset Professor Reeman? He was the most expensive music master money could buy?'

'I think, Aunt, that his talents are so far above mine that he felt we should start off with someone not quite so special, and see how I get on.'

'Well I don't know any third-rate teacher,' Miss Darley said fretfully.

'He did recommend someone; someone who needed the money very badly,' Sandra said, her lids down in case her aunt should see the gleam in her eye. 'He's the organist of a church. Actually I think I would rather like to learn to play a church organ.'

Miss Darley was enchanted to hear that Sandra was about to become enthusiastic about anything. 'Well, child, and so you shall! Rather an unusual talent! Even Audrey can't do that! Oh, now let me think. How long would it take to have an organ erected in the music room?' she fretted.

'Rather a long time, and such a nuisance. Why doesn't the chauffeur drive me to the church? That would be much more convenient. You wouldn't mind, would you? I know you could come with us and hear my starter lessons!'

She was becoming devious, as devious as Richard had said she was. She took an unhappy satisfaction in the thought, especially when Miss Darley hastily said she didn't think she was fit enough to be taken to any church or to sit in discomfort in a pew listening to scales on the organ. Sandra could go alone if she wanted to. Or Lake might accompany her.

'I don't mind either way.' It was the new trick to lull Miss Darley into a sense of having the whip hand, but Sandra despised herself for it.

'Well, that's settled. And then I've got to tell you I've found a top plastic surgeon to do something about that wee scar of yours. My dear, it won't hurt a bit, they tell me! Well, he's only coming to look at it. Just to see what can be done! Indulge me, Sandra, my dear – I have promised myself I will make you as beautiful as Audrey is. Well, she's got everything she wanted out of me and she doesn't come near me and that makes me very upset. Oh, not *upset* upset,' she said hastily. 'Just annoyed enough to do something about it.'

Sandra longed to beg her aunt to leave everyone alone, but she dreaded another upset, another attack. She sat very still and said nothing, thinking about Tony Johnson teaching her organ lessons and making money. At least someone would be gaining from Miss Darley's wealth! Poor Tony, who never complained, and who would never have told Sandra himself that he had two sick relatives to support, out of the meagre earnings of being church organist. Marion, the kindly gossip, had told her, the day they had made apple jelly together.

'I shall make another Will,' Miss Darley said. 'Now don't tell me I've only just signed one. I know I have. But I've just thought of something else I'd like to do with my money. I'll have the solicitors down this very day. Oh, it's going to be such fun. I've had a marvellous thought. No hairdresser has managed to tame that hair of yours, Sandra, pet, so why don't we settle for a wig? A beautiful, red wig. No, a blonde one. Well, we'll see which suits you. And I'll have Laurelle come over from Paris, to make up your face and ... well, child, do look pleased at my plans for you!'

How long was it to go on, Sandra wondered, as she tried and almost managed a smile. But Miss Darley hadn't finished. 'You see, it really is important to make you glamorous and I really can't keep the secret any longer. There is a young man who is interested in you. There!'

Sandra's head shot up. She couldn't keep the surprise out of her face. 'Who, Aunt?' she couldn't stop herself from asking, and everything in her screamed out: don't let it be Richard. Don't let him succumb to temptation and make my aunt feel she's right!

'Ah, I thought that would interest you!' Miss Darley said. 'He hasn't a bean. I'll tell you that before you ask. But he doesn't come empty-handed, so you can't say he wants you just for your money. He has a very old, very important, titled family behind him. He is the Comte de La Turville de Bains. There! How about that! And he is fabulously good-looking, and only in his early thirties.'

The silence between them grew oppressive.

'Well, child, have you nothing to say?' Miss Darley asked sharply, so mindful of the warnings about not letting her aunt get excited or upset, Sandra asked in a reasonable tone, 'It's

216

very interesting, Aunt, but does he know about my limp and scar?'

'Well, of course he doesn't, silly girl! No man would really accept those. That is why I am having the best people take a look at you. I have been assured that both your disabilities can be put right, if the top people get at them. Oh, if only you hadn't gone out with that Benny in his car that day.'

'And when does the Comte see me?' Sandra wanted to know.

'I shall keep putting him off, which will make him all the more eager,' Miss Darley said. 'And it will give me time to get a fabulous wardrobe prepared for you, and one for myself, too,' she finished archly. 'Make very sure I am going to enjoy every minute of it, too.'

Sandra felt so tired when that conversation was finished, that she wished she hadn't pressed the point about Tony giving her lessons. But he was rather nice and would probably listen to all this if not in stupefaction, then at least with real interest. He had already told her that he had seen Audrey and had been fascinated by the wonderful new model her car was.

The lawyers came the next day, just after Sandra had been driven to the church where

Tony was waiting to give the first lesson.

'I say, is that doctor chap around, the one who whisked you off that day? I was pretty fed up about that,' Tony complained. 'I'd almost got the old girl to go. Burst into life the minute your pal moved off.'

'No, he won't come,' Sandra said tautly. 'Not ever again. We had a row, because of my aunt.'

Tony grinned companionably. 'You have my sympathies. Both of you. I wouldn't really like to fall foul of your aunt. Only saw her once, and she said something like "Hey, there, young man, help me, and don't stand with your mouth open!"'

Sandra blushed. 'She never did!'

'Well, I have to admit I'd been playing football with my boys group and I'd only got my oldest sweater and pants on, and I was splashed with mud. Still I did get the feeling that even a dog collar wouldn't have intimidated her!' He grinned at Sandra's dawning smile and took her arm so naturally that she didn't feel he was helping someone with a limp but just being friendly.

'She is going to have me looked at because she doesn't like my scar and limp so I may have to go back into hospital again,' she explained.

'Do you mind?' he asked her, quite seriously.

'I don't have to mind. I have strict medical orders not to upset her so she can get away with anything.'

'Do you really mind, though?' he asked again, and she said, 'Of course I do. I have always said that if someone liked me in spite of everything, I would know it was for myself, so you see, I don't really like making it easy by being made over. I'm to have a wig and make-up, the lot, so if anyone wants to find the real me he'll have to dig deep.' And then they had reached the chancel steps and she was wondering what had made her come.

'I forgot!' she gasped. 'I can't use my leg, so how–'

'Not to worry. The first lesson is a sort of demonstration, and then I'll play to you, a simple little piece, and you can decide if you want to continue. You didn't bring your aunt with you, did you?' he asked anxiously.

'No. She wanted to come, but her lawyers were expected. She's going to change her Will again.'

She settled down to an enjoyable half hour with him, with a brief thought as to what Miss Darley could possibly think of, which merited changing the Will completely instead of just adding a Codicil. Then she gave herself up to hearing Tony play a Bach fugue she had asked for.

Miss Darley had decided already that Sandra would only have one or two lessons, for this new project would take all of her time and Miss Darley's, too. She told her lawyers about it.

They made objections, of course. The freshly signed Will, the one that had so recently been made, left almost everything to Sandra, but a sizeable fortune to Audrey and her new husband. The Will before that, which hadn't been destroyed because Miss Darley had insisted on keeping it herself at the time, and had then gone to hospital, was the one that left everything to Audrey and nothing at all to Sandra. And now, today, it was all going to be reversed, and Audrey herself was to having nothing, nothing. The lawyers didn't like it at all. 'Think, Miss Darley, before you go into this new project!'

They had been warned about not exciting her, but the younger of the two men, in his forties and rather worried about Miss Darley's moods, had forgotten. His uncle looked nervously at her and at his nephew, but the damage had been done. Her face flushed, and she said, 'You don't understand me at all, do you? I always think before I remake a Will, and I have thought well before I remake this one, and to prove it, I shall do this,' and she took the latest Will and tore it across and across again and again and again, until her anger had simmered down. 'Now ... we will make a completely new Will.' She held her heart and looked down at the pieces for a minute, the two men half rising in their seats. Then, summoning everything she had got she reached for her bag, and got out her pills. The younger lawyer got up and poured some water from the drinks tray and without a word, brought the glass over to her and watched while she took the pill. Then her colour began to come back, and she signalled him to sit down again, and for the rest of the discussion and the drafting of the new Will, things were quite peaceful.

'How would if be if we engrossed it here,' the younger man began to suggest, but seeing Miss Darley's mood change, his uncle said, 'Certainly not. We'll do the thing as we always do it for Miss Darley, and send the engrossment through the usual channels tomorrow for signature and witnessing,' and Miss Darley agreed with him.

But she was very tired when they finally

left. She sat looking at the bits of the old Will, and wondered why she had torn it up like that. She should have left that one. If anything happened to her, at least Sandra would have had *something*. Panic seized her. What had she done? With tremendous force of will, she calmed herself. Nothing was going to happen to her. She was strong and fit, and she didn't, she wouldn't let herself, believe that there was really anything wrong with her heart, that is, if nobody upset her. She spent the rest of the day quietly, playing cards with Sandra – a very subdued Sandra – in the evening, and retiring to bed with a serene smile. She had had her own way, hadn't she? She was getting her own way from everyone, at last, at the end of a very stormy battle-filled life, and because of the threat of her heart, everyone was giving in to her, and quite right too. But might it not just be a little dull, a small voice inside her protested, if she could never have a single small argument? If there had to be complete agreement with her all the time, every time?

She stood briefly at the window, looking out at the night. The sky was like a dark blue velvet cloth that had once been spread to show off a diamond necklace a jeweller was trying to sell her. She had liked the cloth better than the diamonds, and in the end, she hadn't bought them. What an odd thing to think! She had been put to bed by Miss Lake, and took childish pleasure in getting out of bed again, once she was alone, just to look at the night sky. But never before had she felt so lonely. She could only suppose it was because she now had no way of knowing if people liked her. Their calming, yet false, smiles and affable manner, told her nothing. She was frightened. She had a power over them, by virtue of that shaky heart of hers, but it was a back-kicking power: she didn't know friend from foe, and above all, she needed to know if Sandra was her foe. She decided she'd ring for the child. She forgot Sandra's leg, and how it hurt her to make the journey from her room to her aunt's. Unlike the thoughtful vicar and his wife Marion, nobody at Darley House had thought to make available to Sandra a downstairs room, and in any case, she would have had to go upstairs to her aunt's room at times like this. Miss Darley just needed to get across to that bell-rope and pull it. But all of a sudden it seemed a long way away, and the hush-hush sound of the little wind moving the leaves in the trees near her open window sounded very much louder and there was a drum thudding in her ears, which she finally realised was the urgent quickening beat of her tired old heart. She couldn't breathe, couldn't call out, and she felt lost in an alien world. She fell a long, long way, although it was only to the floor, and the last thing she tried to say was, 'Sandra...' Miss Lake – hovering near the suite of rooms because she wasn't sure her mistress intended to keep in bed – heard her name torn from her lips before the crash of her body met the floor.

Richard had been watching that same sky, but thinking about Sandra. Had her aunt been telling the truth? He liked to argue against himself when he had time, and now he asked himself, suppose Sandra had been telling the truth? That made her aunt the liar, and what reason could make her tell such a lie? Well, according to Miss Darley's beliefs, it would be very wrong of her to leave everything to one niece and not to the other, so it was on the cards that she had split the fortune and left half to each girl and thought nothing wrong was in that. And perhaps because Sandra had this strange idea, which probably Miss Darley associated with Sandra's accident, or just her old wilfulness coming out, Miss Darley decided to do what she herself wanted with her own money, and made it public that Sandra was to have things as she wanted them. Pleasing everyone, Richard thought sardonically, and not being able to resist boasting about her cleverness, to Richard himself. But she had said that Sandra knew and agreed to the subterfuge...

The arguments swayed in his mind and wouldn't work out, and in the end he groaned and put his hot forehead on the cool glass of the pane, and recognised what he should have recognised from the start: it didn't matter what part Sandra had played in it all, it didn't matter whether she had told the truth or not been open with him. The clear cold fact of the matter was that Sandra was under his skin. He loved her helplessly and there was not a thing he could do about it. He wouldn't accept her money, so it meant that he would have to go through life without her, and meantime get used to the agony of knowing that she was the only one in the world for him.

A car slowed down in the road. He straightened up. It would be his father's car at last. He hurried downstairs, but there was no longer a car there: it had just been someone else slowing down. A little nagging doubt began to creep into his mind, yet he still told himself not to worry about his father. He had wanted to drive over to the coast with Philippa and Richard himself had not protested, out of despair. He knew, his friend the consultant who was to look at his father, knew also, that Dr Norwood Senr. had left things too long. They would operate, but without much hope. So Richard had made no protest, but allowed his father to take the car out today with Philippa. Philippa had become more amenable since he had told her how ill his father was. Sometimes he was afraid Philippa was just biding her time, before she started showing Richard how much she wanted him, sometimes he thought that Philippa was really happy to be with his father. She was a strange girl, one could never be certain what she was thinking. But she was hard: Richard had seen that for himself. He didn't think she really cared about his father's prognosis.

He forced himself to think of his father and Philippa, so that he wouldn't have to think about Sandra, but it wasn't possible. Although it was getting late, he couldn't keep his mind on where his father might be. He kept thinking of Sandra's limp, wondering if anything could be done about it. And that scar. It wasn't a big one, but it hurt him to think of that dear face with any sort of blemish. Not that Sandra herself cared. He began to wonder what she herself felt about all this, and the gnawing urge to telephone her and talk this over with her took possession of him. Would she talk to him, at this time of night? He didn't know what Darley House was like, but unlike Miss Darley, he thought at once of how long and how painful the journey from her room to the telephone might be. He decided against it, and stood there aimlessly in the hall of his father's house, wondering what to do. He couldn't bring himself to go to bed until his father had returned, but he didn't want to see Philippa.

Hell, his father was a grown man. He wouldn't thank his son for worrying about him. Richard decided to go to bed. And his sleepless mind suddenly succumbed to pressures, once his head touched the pillow, and he slept.

Such deep sleep was inevitable, since he had had a lot of sleepless nights lately, and had taken on extra duties to repay colleagues who had let him get away when Sandra was so ill. He slept too deeply even to dream. The telephone had been ringing persistently for some time before it got through to him and he awoke fuzzily just as it stopped.

Automatically he called up his hospital to know if they had been trying to get him, but they hadn't, so he replaced the receiver. But now he was awake, he got up, and found it was well after midnight. The house was so still and quiet. He had the odd sensation that Sandra was needing him, that something was wrong at Darley House. He telephoned his uncle, then remembered they had gone away on holiday, and the house was occupied by the clergyman from Wales who had come to take over. He hastily replaced the receiver before he awoke a strange household.

But he couldn't go to bed again. He dressed and, thinking, looked into his father's room. The bed had not been slept in. The door of Philippa's room was open, and she was not there. They really shouldn't be out as late as this. Then the reason for the telephone call struck him: they had probably decided to stay over at some hotel, and were ringing to tell him, he told himself. He wanted to believe that, but it was highly unlikely. His heart started to quicken its beat. There could only be one reason for that telephone call...

Cars break down, he told himself, but it wasn't possible for his father to keep a car out until after midnight for it to break down. His father knew he was a sick man. Besides, Philippa was with him. She liked to go to bed early. She would have hammered at him to return much sooner than this. She would have hammered at him...

Richard pulled on a thick sweater and went out of the house, checked (rather foolishly, he thought) that the car wasn't in the garage, and then ran out into the quiet street. He had to look up and down the road, though for what reason, he couldn't say. It was a normally busy street that the doctor's house was on, but at this time the traffic quietened. At this moment there was no movement but the stealthy speeding across the road of a cat going home. A sense of disaster clamped down on him, which was strange. He was the most cool and level-headed of persons. He forced himself to return to the house, and as he did so, the telephone started to ring again.

It was not Nosterwell Hospital, but the one in Huddlestone. About his father...

NINE

Richard didn't believe in miracles. He was convinced that his father had left things too late, with his own ailment. Their two consultant friends had said the same. But his father had been whipped up to theatre for his injuries in the accident, long before Richard arrived. So, too, had Philippa, although hers had been considerably less serious than those of his father.

'What happened?' he had asked.

There were conflicting reports. One witness said that they were talking and didn't see the lorry coming towards them. Another witness said the lorry swerved right across the road at them and they would have been able to do nothing. Richard, who now had the practice to run, was forced to go home, and before he could go to bed, he had an urgent call from one of his father's old patients. Old Ebenezer Kellett, whose centuries-old cottage was just outside the town, and who insisted not only in living alone in it, but keeping his bed in an upstairs rom. Predictably he fell often down the narrow stairs.

'Where's my old friend Jim, eh?' the old man wheezed to Richard.

'My father wasn't able to come,' Richard said kindly, as he helped the neighbour carry the old man up to his bedroom. 'You've fallen downstairs again. Why don't you have your bed moved downstairs?'

'Because this house of mine mightn't look much but it's three hundred year old and more and it's going to be treated with respect it deserves, and no sleeping in the setting-rooms,' the old man muttered.

He was in pain but he wouldn't admit it. Richard gently examined him and said finally, 'Well, I'm afraid you are going to have to do something about your scruples, Mr Kellett, because you've done something a bit more serious this time and I'm going to have to ship you off to hospital.'

The old man was really upset. 'No, no, don't take me away from this place,' he begged. 'Young 'ns 'll get in and smash everything. They come and call out that old place should be knocked down, as it is. Don't, *don't* send me away!'

'Well, I'll have to take you to hospital to have you put in plaster, but I'll see they bring you back immediately after. You've broken a bone,' he insisted gently.

'Old bones snap at my age,' he muttered, but he agreed, so Richard called the ambulance, left the neighbour promising to stay there till they returned, and went with old Mr Kellett to have his leg set. There wasn't a bed free to admit him, anyway, so Richard brought him back again, installed him comfortably, the neighbour's wife promising to look in on him, and then Richard went back home to snatch a couple of hours sleep before the next call came. This was a difficult twin birth up at the farm on the hill, and it was well after breakfast time that he had finished, both twins doing well but the mother very weak. His first confinement in his father's practice.

The farmer insisted that Richard should stay for a good breakfast, which he did, though he nearly fell asleep over it.

While he ate, the farmer stayed to have more strong tea with him. 'I had it in mind to have a word with you, doctor. Well, your father, actually, and I'm right sorry to hear about his accident. But as you're carrying on then I must say it to you. I can't pay the bill, doctor.'

Richard forced his thoughts away from his father. He should have telephoned the hospital. They might have been trying to get him. Briefly he found himself wishing Philippa had been at home to mind the telephone, then he hastily amended that thought, with some alarm. Philippa, in her present mood, would merely have added to his troubles.

'Let's talk about the bill later,' Richard said hastily.

'No, we won't, then. We'll discuss it now. What I thought was, I'll not owe you doctor. It's not in me to owe anyone.'

Richard stared. How, then, was this conversation going to work out? The farmer explained. 'I'll pay you in kind. Everyone wants food. A side of bacon, and eggs regular every week, something like that, till it's paid like. How would that suit you?'

'That should do fine! Is that how my father–?' he began, then broke off. He shouldn't have said that.

The farmer grinned. 'Maybe. I wouldn't know. Healthy, here, we are, but I always said if I needed doctor, I'd pay my way, not go and queue up in the waiting-room. Call him out if I needed him, that's my way. Still, healthy we may be, but it's the start of the family, and maybe next year I'll do the same, if you're willing. Right, send in your bill, doctor, and I'll see you get your value.'

Before Richard got through to the hospital, he had seen two more patients – both of the same way of thinking and with bills owing. One of them insisted on paying with a pair of silver candlesticks. The other – an elderly maiden lady who was deeply distressed over the matter, but proud – sent Richard away with a beautifully embroidered tea cloth by way of payment. And the hospital had a further bonus for him. Incredibly, his father was doing nicely, they said.

'While we had him on the table, we discovered something else and whipped it out,' the young surgeon said cheerfully. Then, sensing Richard's surprise, he said, 'It was benign! No bother! He'll be fine, but no more calls in the night for him for some time. Six months rest, I'd say.'

Richard felt so weak, he sat down suddenly. Philippa, he was further told, was also doing nicely, and apparently hadn't asked to see him. Shakily he returned the receiver to its hook, made himself some coffee, and felt much better when surgery opened.

'How's your father? We've heard!' every patient said, one after another. He hadn't realised his father was thought so much of. One woman said, 'It's a miracle, it really is! But there, your father was only saying to me last week, nobody knows for sure till they have a good look, what's there, and it won't necessarily be the worst kind of news,' she finished delicately. 'Now I shan't mind going in for my operation!'

When surgery closed, he went to see his father. Dr Norwood looked smaller somehow, in bed, and Richard was only allowed a minute or two. His father said weakly, 'Surprise, eh?' as if he had realised what Richard had been dreading. 'You never know!'

Richard nodded, speechlessly.

'How are you managing, Richard?'

Richard smiled broadly and said, 'Fine! Paying their bills, too,' and his father said, 'In kind, I suppose,' so that made it all right. 'Will you carry on for me till I'm back?'

Richard was about to say an easy 'Yes, of course,' when his father looked straight at him. It was a question that had to be faced properly, here and now, at this stage, if his father were going to make a good recovery. Here was no easy fobbing off with a facile affirmative. Richard faced his leaving the hospital, and his hopes of research, in a lightning moment, while his father waited. Research? Well, he couldn't afford it. And the hospital? No, it would have to go. His father couldn't carry on. He just wouldn't be fit enough for months and months.

'Yes. It's all right with the hospital. I've thought about it. I'll take over, so don't you worry about a thing. I expect you can do with a partner, anyway, when you're back!' and he was rewarded with the sort of relieved smile that his father hadn't given him since he was a boy.

Visits to Philippa were necessarily rushed, as the practice was surprisingly busy and Philippa surprisingly quiet and undemanding. He did ask them closely how she was progressing, but he was assured that it was as her notes said: no problems, quiet steady progress. Then why hadn't she created a scene at first sight of him, he asked himself worriedly?

He literally hadn't time to worry. He sent her some flowers (from the garden) but he didn't know her taste in reading, so he made no attempt at sending magazines. He told the ward sister to let him know if there was anything she wanted, then departed with the usual rush of the average G.P., back to the hectic life of the practice and a car that wasn't always certain to behave properly.

His father was going to be a long job in hospital, but evidently Philippa would be up and about soon, and there his worries started to grow. What could he do with her? There was only one chap he could think of at the hospital who might help: Charlie Pearce who owed Richard a favour, and had a mother who adored invalids to fuss over. Richard found to his surprise that Lady Pearce had been visiting Philippa already; not surprising as she usually did a round of those people without visitors. She seemed to have taken to Philippa, and gladly offered to have her stay at her home in a country village in the other direction, for which Richard weakly breathed a silent prayer of relief. He could now put his father's mind at rest, and also his own.

'By the way,' Charlie said, 'don't you want to hear the big news? About your heiress?'

Richard stiffened. Sandra, who lived at the back of his mind, and haunted him without cessation... 'What about her?' he forced himself to say.

'You must have heard the old lady died suddenly in the night, the same night as your father's accident, actually! She'd arranged for a big noise to come over from the States, expressly to do something about that limp of her niece's, and he's come! Here! How's that? Boy, is he hot stuff!'

'Oh, I did hear something. I didn't realise it was for her,' Richard said, and his heart sank. So Sandra had lied, after all. She was the heiress! Only a very great deal of money could have procured *that* man's services, or brought him over to this country at such short notice.

'Well, don't you want to hear what happened? He was made to have a bash and reckons he's pulled it off. Well, she's up on her pins again, getting around already.'

'I'm glad,' Richard said, but he felt so shaken inside, that all he wanted to do was to get away somewhere and think about her, without anyone seeing what was showing with naked truth in his face. So she was rich, so that was goodbye to Sandra!

'That's not all,' Charlie said with relish. 'She's also going to have plastic surgery for that scar on her face. They reckon that'll be in the bag too. Some folks have all the luck, eh?'

'I'm glad,' Richard said again, and wondered how it was that his friend couldn't see what his news had done. All through the surgery that day Richard wrestled with the thought that whatever else, Sandra might be able to move about again with the old verve and gusto, and that face of hers would crinkle up in the sheer joy of living, as he remembered it. How could old Miss Darley have thought her niece Sandra wasn't beautiful? Richard had never seen such a lovely face, he thought. He had wanted to stare at it all the time, but she had never been for him, not since he had learned her connection with Darley House.

That day his Aunt Marion telephoned him, ostensibly about his father, but it became apparent very soon that it was really about Sandra. 'I did wonder, dear, if you had heard about her newest operation? Oh, silly of me, of course you would, from your old hospital. Well, I mean, wouldn't you?'

'Yes, I did hear, Aunt Marion.'

'I wanted to go and see her, but the car's out of action again,' Marion said, and waited.

'I'm sorry, my dear,' he said, 'but I'm run off my feet with the practice. I've left the hospital, you know.'

'Yes, I thought you might have,' she said slowly, then for some reason he couldn't understand, she rang off.

Odd, for her to behave like that. He went back to the patient sitting by him waiting, and this time he couldn't push Sandra out of his mind. It was the connection with his

Aunt Marion, he supposed. He kept seeing Sandra that first day, laughing about her tumble off the bike, laughing as she played with the puppies and kittens at the Rectory, laughing and happy all the time until ... yes, he remembered, with sudden sharpness, yes, she had stopped being laughing and happy the very first time it struck her that he would be wanting to drive her right home to her own front door. And she hadn't been open and frank with him since.

During the morning he was able to push her right from his mind. One of the twins at the farm had a high temperature. That morning was another hectic one, finishing with his having to admit the baby to the hospital. If it had been the little mother, he caught himself thinking, he wouldn't have been surprised. But this was the large twin of the two ... it didn't make sense.

That twin occupied his mind so much that when he heard it was out of danger some days later, he felt he just had to go over to the hospital baby unit and see for himself. He had often heard his father say that babies threw up an alarm like that, then pulled out of it, and succumbed to a final attack when one least expected it. Somehow it was most necessary that these twins, above all babies, should survive and flourish. His first delivery in his father's practice and it just had to go right.

The young nurse took him into the big sunny nursery. All the babies were squalling. 'They know the time better than we do!' the girl laughed and went on with her preparations, leaving him to find the baby he wanted, and to satisfy himself that it was all right. He was standing there with it in his arms when a voice he knew well from the open door to the next room, said suddenly, 'I've done this one! Any more?' and Sandra appeared, in her dressing-gown, a fat red-faced baby cuddled to her shoulder. She saw Richard and for a moment he thought she might drop the baby. He felt like dropping the one he held. They stood and stared at each other. An older nurse came and quietly took the baby from him, and returned it to its cot, then went to take Sandra's.

'Perhaps you'd like to go in the next room, doctor, while we do these,' the older nurse suggested.

Sandra turned and walked – almost perfectly, but painfully slowly – ahead of him. He wanted to rush to her and support her but he didn't, and she knew he was behind her watching her progress, and it took everything she had, not to let that bad leg give way. She collapsed into her low seat and looked up at him, wishing she had managed to stay standing.

He sat down on another low chair near her. 'Hello,' he said.

'Hello,' she said, and pulling herself together, added, 'I heard about your father, from Mrs Vennall. I'm sorry. How is he?'

'He's fine. Well, a lot better than I expected. And he's going to recover.'

'And you're running the practice?' It was a question, and she wanted to know so badly if Philippa were home, keeping house for him.

'Trying to,' he said, 'and getting indigestion from the good-natured but not very efficient cooking of our next door neighbour,' which answered her question up to a point. So Philippa wasn't at home with him, but no doubt would be when she recovered sufficiently. And what would happen then?

'I'm so glad things are going well with you,' he said awkwardly.

'Well yes,' she said, surprised. 'I was jolly lucky to have a promise of a job in the baby wing. Just while I'm getting around. Then I'm going to try again for a limited nurse's training. Not an S.R.N. I don't think I've got the brains for that.'

'Why should you want to take up nursing? *Now*, I mean?'

'I must do something to earn my bread,' she said, shrugging a little.

'Earn your bread? But I don't understand!'

'You did know that my aunt had died suddenly?'

He nodded, so she said, 'Well, I didn't know, of course, exactly what had happened, but apparently she lost her temper with her solicitors and tore up the existing Will because she was making another one leaving everything to me.'

'I know that,' he said coldly.

'No, you don't! There were two Wills – one cutting me out altogether, that I told you about and you wouldn't believe. Then when I went home with her this last time she'd made another, I think giving Audrey and me half each. I didn't know about that, but I believe she told you about it.'

He didn't answer. Distressed, she perceived she had lost the advantage, but she pressed on.

'Well, my aunt hadn't destroyed the earlier one cutting me out. I think in the excitement they all forgot it. Then she wanted to make a third Will, leaving everything to me and cutting Audrey out altogether, and the lawyers were going away to engross it for signature. Everyone thought she was so much better, but she died in the night without signing the last Will, so the earlier one (the one cutting me out altogether) was the one that stood. Well, it would, wouldn't it?'

She watched him anxiously. It was essential that he should believe her, but there was still something he didn't understand. 'Sandra, your surgeon from America must have cost the earth to fetch over here.'

'You won't trust me or believe me, will you? I don't have to tell you this, but the fact is that Audrey is so rich – well, she very kindly said she'd pay for the two things my Aunt wanted so much – my leg surgery and my face. If they didn't come off, I was to go and live with her.' She shuddered at the thought, and Richard, cursing himself for not believing her, could quite well see that Audrey would be glad to foot these bills, if only to be sure there would be no invalid cousin in her own home all the time.

'I think I'll go back to my ward,' Sandra said, struggling to get up, but the seat was a low nursing one and she wasn't quite able to do that much alone yet, and the nearness of

Richard confused her so that she almost fell sideways off it in her efforts to hurry. He caught her arms, raised her to her full height, and had forgotten what a little thing she was. 'Sandra…' he began thickly. 'Sandra, love, I'm *sorry*. Forgive? Oh, I've wanted you so badly,' and he buried his face in her hair.

Vaguely he realised it had been cut very short and neat, and he missed the spiky bits that used to stick up on end. 'What have they done to you?' he asked, moving his face round till his mouth found hers.

When she could speak, after a long kiss that seemed to take all the strength out of her and to leave her rather light-headed, she said, 'Audrey also wanted to stand me a beautician's course – my aunt wanted it so badly. I'd got used to giving in to my aunt, so I let Audrey take me in hand, only I got tired of it before we progressed very far.'

'Don't let her do anything else for you. I love you as you are!' he said.

After a silence, she said, 'Richard, say that again!' So he did, several times. The older nurse came in and hastily backed out again, for they were still standing there locked in each other's arms, oblivious of the world around them or of the squalling babies in the next room.

'I love you so much, I was at a point where I would have asked you to marry me in spite of your money, much as I am against inherited wealth. Do you know what it is to ache for someone, to never be able to put them out of your mind? Do you?'

'Yes, oh yes, I do. You must know I do, after that day at your aunt's with you.'

'Your birthday!' he said, remembering. 'And you've never given me a thought since – confess it!'

'Because I let a man pick me up and because I went in Benny's car and got in a crash? One doesn't have to be alone to be miserable. I wanted people with me, but they didn't help. My aunt wanted me to marry a French count with a great title and a castle and no money at all, and I think I'd have said yes to him, I missed you so much it was like toothache.'

'Marry me, Sandra? I haven't any money. I'm running my father's practice and it's a dog's life. Calls in the small hours, no peace at all. And the bills are paid by sides of bacon and lace tablecloths.'

That made her laugh, and in putting her head back, she realised that the reason for the muted note of the babies' crying was because the communicating door had been quietly shut. 'We'd better go, Richard. What must they think?'

'I don't care what they think. I've asked you a question I'll never have the nerve to repeat, so I must have the answer now, love. Will you?'

'Of course I will, if you want me, really want *me*, with no money, nothing at all. Not even Darley House – that was left to a charity because Audrey hated it.'

'It's the only way I wanted you, dear love, with nothing, so I could give you things. I could have, with my hospital job, but now I can't. Not even a roof over my head, without asking my father.'

'That part's all right, but what about Philippa?' She had to know.

'I'm just not thinking about it. A friend of mine is taking her to his home to recuperate.'

'He's keen on her?' Sandra asked eagerly.

Richard looked startled. 'I shouldn't think so. It's his mother who likes her. I wish old Charlie would get keen on her, but I doubt that. He's a confirmed bachelor.' He kissed Sandra lingeringly again. 'I'll take you back to your ward. We're in the way here, I think. And I must get back to the surgery. Dear love, I'll hate leaving you here. Let's find out how soon you're due for release.'

She didn't want him to take her all the way. Remembering her reluctance to be taken back to Darley House, he said, 'Why not, love? You must be honest with me now, or it will all have been for nothing. All that terrible time when I didn't know what was going on or why you wouldn't tell me about it.'

'You won't like it!' Sandra said roundly. 'I'm in William and Mary Wing.' She nodded as his face changed. 'I knew you'd hate it. How can I help it? Audrey insisted. She's splashing money around on me because she feels terrible having got the lot and I've got nothing. Honestly, nothing would please her more if she could hear that I'd married someone with a lot of money. That way she could wash her hands of me and go off and enjoy her own fortune.'

'Well, she won't be given that pleasure, love, will she?' Richard said with a lot of satisfaction. In spite of his loathing of inherited wealth, he was very angry that his Sandra had been left nothing, after the way her aunt had messed things up for himself and Sandra.

But Audrey did get the pleasure, although it was some time afterwards. Dr Norwood Senr. was home, unlikely to do much in the practice again but fit enough to enjoy a quiet life with his son carrying on. Philippa had, much to everyone's astonishment, enchanted not only Lady Pearce, but Charlie, too, and they had had a quiet wedding and she wasn't coming back to the doctor's house again. Richard said, 'We'd better get married then, now you're over your plastic surgery, Sandra, because Dad and I feel we won't survive our neighbour's cooking much longer!'

'What a proposal!' she retorted.

It was a very quiet wedding at the local church, but the economical week-end at Huddlestone had to be postponed, because the locum let them down and they couldn't get anyone else at short notice. And while they were raising their glasses to Sandra, who, under her big white flowered picture hat, looked as beautiful as Richard had dreamed of her, they had a visit from a business-like city type with a briefcase, who was much confused when he realised he'd blundered in on a small wedding reception.

'I've come about the cottage of the late Ebenezer Kellett,' he announced. 'I'm sorry if I've come at a rather special moment, but I think you'll be glad to hear my news, and then I'll take myself off.'

'Who's Ebenezer Kellett?' Sandra whispered, her face puckered with laughter. All her old gaiety had returned since she had been discharged from hospital after successful plastic surgery.

'Oh, I forgot to tell you,' Richard said. 'It's the poor old boy who wouldn't have his bed put on the ground floor because his home was three hundred years old. He didn't survive his last fall downstairs.'

'Yes, well,' the solicitor said, 'he left special witnessed instructions as to how all his debts should be paid up by his few possessions, and as your bill was the largest, doctor, you get the cottage. It's in a bad state, I'm afraid, but yes, it is really three hundred years old, if that means anything.'

He left after he had drunk to the bride, and then Richard's father said, 'Well, what do I want with a cottage? I'd better give it to you two for a wedding present.'

It was, as they found out later, rather in need of repair, which was a pity. Richard remembered white walls and heavy black beams, a pointed top to the heavy front door and giant hinges with raised nails; and the windows, he thought, had been diamond paned. But it had been dark and he had been tired and thinking only of the patient.

But it had been a gem of a place.

Inside the cottage they found linenfold panelling in the room the old man wouldn't have his bed put into, and there was woodworm. The beautiful tongued wood floors were badly in need of cleaning and polishing, and the staircase with its banister posts and newel posts of carved bishops, was splitting in places. At the back, woefully over-run with weeds to the point of almost excluding the original lay-out, there was a perfect Elizabethan garden, with hedges that had once been clipped into fantastic shapes, and a sundial in the middle of the crossing point of four paved walks. The garden beds had once been cut into formal patterns but were now almost past doing anything with. 'What a shame! It must have been beautiful once!' Sandra breathed. 'Oh, couldn't we live here and put it right, gradually?'

Richard didn't answer, but Sandra was dismayed at his expression. 'Now don't you dare say I'm talking like an heiress, because I never did talk like that! I never once got what I wanted myself, so I'm not missing anything. It's just that ... oh, one doesn't often see such a lovely Tudor relic. It's wicked, letting it go like this.'

'We can't live here. No time to work on it.

Too far from the practice. We'd better ask Dad if he minds us selling it, get what we can, to put by. We must have something saved. I've had too many jolts lately not to want a little money behind me.'

'All right,' Sandra sighed. 'Are you sure I can't train as a nurse?'

But Richard was adamant. 'My wife is not going to work,' he said with finality. 'Besides, you may not be able to,' he said, in a tone that made Sandra blush, as he started kissing her. 'I don't want you away from me,' he said fiercely, between kisses. 'I've ached for you so much. I'd be afraid of losing you again. Come on, let's get home and talk to Dad about this.'

In the event, Sandra discovered that she would not be able to work at anything. They were so much in love, and so soon a baby was on the way. Sandra was so happy. For the first time in her life things were going her way. Even the pregnancy – unlike Audrey's – was going fine. And about that time, an offer was made for the Elizabethan cottage.

It was a telephone offer. Dr Norwood and Sandra heard Richard say, 'I can't believe it! Would you mind repeating that?' Then he covered the receiver and said blankly, 'He says the first Elizabeth once sheltered there in a storm. He wants to take it down stone by stone and ship it to the States and rebuild it,' and then he told them the price offered.

His father said briskly, 'If this chap's got so much money, for heaven's sake snap the offer up, boy, and stop sounding surprised,' so Richard did.

Later, much later, after evening surgery, as they walked in the cool of the doctor's neat but uninspiring back garden, Richard said, 'My lovely wife, I shall be able to provide for you after all. I shall be almost rich.'

'Well!' Sandra exploded. 'I never thought I'd hear you say that, after all the fuss you made about the possibility of me being rich!'

'That was inherited wealth. This has been earned – it's in lieu of fees. Besides, what chap wants a rich wife? Although I can confess now, that I was almost on the point of coming to propose to you in spite of your money, I wanted you so badly. You'd have branded me as an adventurer!'

'No, it would have been the conquest I always said I wanted,' she told him, between kisses.

'A conquest of me, that would have been,' he said severely. 'Me and my principles! That wasn't the idea at all!'

'Well, now you've conquered me. Well, either way, it was a very sweet conquest,' she murmured, before succumbing to the drowning sensation of her beloved Richard's kisses.